John T Dale

What Ben Beverly Saw at the Great Exposition

John T Dale

What Ben Beverly Saw at the Great Exposition

ISBN/EAN: 9783337418465

Printed in Europe, USA, Canada, Australia, Japan

Cover: Foto ©Andreas Hilbeck / pixelio.de

More available books at **www.hansebooks.com**

What Ben Beverly Saw

AT THE

GREAT EXPOSITION.

BY A CHICAGO LAWYER.

—WITH—

THE NATIONAL ODE,
BY BAYARD TAYLOR,

—AND—

THE CENTENNIAL ORATION,
BY HON. W. M. EVARTS.

Illustrated with Numerous Full-page Engravings.

CHICAGO:
MOSES WARREN & CO., 103 STATE ST.
1877.

TO

THE AMERICAN PEOPLE,

WHOSE MATCHLESS ENTERPRISE, DAUNTLESS HEROISM, UNFLINCHING PATRIOTISM

AND WISE EDUCATIONAL SYSTEM, HAVE CREATED, IN A CENTURY, THE

GREATEST OF REPUBLICS, THIS BOOK IS RESPECTFULLY DEDICATED,

BY THE AUTHOR, IN COMMEMORATION OF THE FIRST CEN-

TENNIAL ANNIVERSARY OF OUR NATIONAL LIFE; WITH

THE HOPE THAT IT MAY INSPIRE A GREATER LOVE

OF COUNTRY, AND A CLOSER FEELING OF

UNIVERSAL BROTHERHOOD AMONG ALL

WHO MAY PERUSE ITS PAGES.

TABLE OF CONTENTS.

DEDICATION.

INTRODUCTION.

WORLD TREASURES OF THE MAIN BUILDING.

CONTENTS.

CONTENTS.

THE ANNEX TO THE MAIN BUILDING.

NEW ENGLAND IN THE OLDEN TIME.

UNCLE SAM'S GOVERNMENT BUILDING.

CONTENTS.

CONTENTS.

THE BEAUTIFUL ALGERIAN.

MARVELS OF AGRICULTURAL HALL.

OUR SCHOOLS AND SOME OTHERS.

THE TURKISH CAFE.

HORTICULTURAL HALL.

CASTELLANI COLLECTION OF ANCIENT CURIOSITIES.

PRE-HISTORIC RACES AND RELICS.

ODDS AND ENDS; HERE AND THERE.

STUDIES FROM THE ART GALLERY.

Being vivid and graphic pen-pictures describing the following remarkable works of Art, grouped in topics and chapters.

SOUL IN COLORS.

STUDIES OF THE BEAUTIFUL.

GLIMPSES OF THE HORRIBLE.

LIST OF FULL PAGE ILLUSTRATIONS.

INTRODUCTION.

DEAR READER:

If you will throw aside your cares and anxieties, smooth the wrinkles from your brow, and drive the shadows from your heart, I will accompany you to the great Centennial Exposition, at Philadelphia — not by rushing trains or crowded omnibuses, but, perusing these pages—in the quiet seclusion of your homes, by your firesides, in your moments of leisure, or hours of travel, in your parlor, study, or wherever you will. Perhaps you have already been there; then it shall be my pleasant privilege, to refresh your memories, and awaken to new life your enthusiasm, in reviewing the objects of beauty and interest you witnessed there, and also to compare notes with you. If you have not been, and cannot go, except in imagination with me, I will use my best endeavor to repair what you lose, by making your impressions of it, as real and vivid as possible. This event is an epoch in our history, worthy of our careful notice. Bayard Taylor, who has witnessed all the great world's fairs, expresses the opinion, that taken as a whole, our Exposition surpasses all its predecessors.

With this short introduction, and your consent to visit or review this wonderful gathering of the nations, we will begin our journey at once, by first examining:—

PHILADELPHIA U.S. AMERICA
1776
1876
MAY 10TH NOVEMBER 10TH 1876.
INTERNATIONAL EXHIBITION
MAIN EXHIBITION BUILDING.

The World Treasures of the Main Building.

It is impossible for words to convey any adequate idea of the extent and richness of the display in this department of the Exposition. Suppose, in imagination, you accompany me through this vast wilderness of beauty, and we will attempt to get a general idea of the whole, and to notice in detail, many of the most remarkable objects. And first, let us ascend the organ gallery, at the end of the building, and, looking down the entire length of the hall, we see before us a brilliant and exhilarating spectacle,—flags, tapestries, laces, statuary, beautiful show-cases by the acre, filled with the finest manufactured goods of all descriptions; so much, that it is possible only to generalize. We see a vast room, about one-third of a mile in length, and three hundred and fifty feet wide, filled with the finest products of man's skill and industry, from all parts of the world. Here and there, in large black letters on a scarlet ground, appears the name of each country represeuted. Let us descend, and pass through the labyrinths of aisles, and notice more particularly some of the most striking exhibits; and first, we will begin at home. Our own country, many supposed, was indifferent, and even neg-ligent in sending articles for exhibition, but a very few mo-ments of observation, convinces one that this impression is entirely without foundation.

As a people, we may well be proud of our department; and to thousands from abroad, it will be a wonderful revelation. Here are acres covered with almost every conceivable product of industry, of the finest quality and shown to the best ad-vantage. To enumerate, would be to give a catalogue of all manufactures. And not only the most common and substan-tial articles of daily use, but also those costly and delicate attendants of luxury, which our foreign neighbors have sup-posed, that only they, with their generations of skillful ex-perience, could produce in perfection. The old world has long admitted the superiority of our reaping and threshing machines, and labor-saving machinery; but explains it on the ground of necessity,—that we have lacked laborers, and were obliged to resort to machinery as a substitute. But a careful examination must convince all, that the world contains no fingers more cunning, no minds more inventive, nor tastes more refined, than are found on our shores. For instance, notice those magnificent pianos, which stand unrivalled in

THE CENTURY VASE. (p. 14.)

the whole world; these cameos of the most exquisite workmanship,—this, for example, representing the ancient Briton in his
war chariot, his three horses flying like the wind, every part of
which, when examined under a magnifying glass, shows a
finish and accuracy which is truly wonderful; or this set of
jewelry in five pieces, designed for the descendants of John
Alden and Priscilla, whom Longfellow has immortalized in
his poem, "The Courtship of Miles Standish," which is made
by placing pieces of the veritable Plymouth Rock in gold set-
tings of beautiful design; or this necklace, blazing with a
score of brilliant diamonds, worth $42,000; or these sets of
furniture which almost belong to the realm of the fine arts,
and which are fit for palaces of the proudest monarchs; and
we have reason to take pride in the high rank of our
skilled labor in its most artistic aspect.

Let us notice this mantel made from Mexican onyx, for the
Emperor of Germany, by a New York house, which is a marvel of beauty, not only in regard to the material, but also in
design and finish.   In front, are two columns with silver trimmings; on the top stands a neat clock, with antique design
in silver, in bas-relief.   This marble is light colored, dappled
with different shades in the most exquisite manner, and extremely rich and delicate in its appearance.   The price of
this household treasure was $2500.

One of the most exquisite pieces of workmanship, is a **vase** called "The Century Vase," made by the Gorham Company, the celebrated manufacturers of silver ware. It is about five feet long, and four feet high, and contains two thousand ounces of solid silver. It is an epitome of our history during the last century; so suggestive and appropriate are the designs.

Here are copies of celebrated statuary in terra-cotta, which do so much to popularize art, and to cultivate the taste of thousands, who, otherwise, would have no conception of the master pieces of famous artists. Here is Diana by Benzoni, the Apollo Belvidere from the Vatican at Rome, the ancient Warwick vase from the British Museum, an Egyptian vase of great antiquity, and many other copies of noted art treasures. In a show case containing military uniforms and accoutrements, we notice a fine wax figure of Marshall Mac Mahon of France, which, judged by his portraits, must be a strikingly accurate likeness. A well built, military figure, a fine face with dignified commanding expression, gray hair and mustache, and the mien of one "born to command."

The American Bible Society, exhibit specimens of their bibles, printed in two hundred different languages. They have John Milton's Bible, which is yellow from age, and yet well preserved, It is a small edition, about five inches long, and three wide, in red morocco and gilt. They have also a

HEBE. (p. 14.)

large bible printed in Venice in 1476, and its pages are like a field spangled with bright flowers, so gayly colored are the illuminations.

In a department containing school-books and dictionaries, we find a specimen of the handwriting of Noah Webster, the author of Webster's Dictionary. It is a leaf or two from his manuscript of the dictionary, written in a plain, old fashioned hand, in a labored manner, a large portion of it erased and interlined. It makes one ache to think of the long years of constant, steady toil, required to write such a dictionary as his, in such an exact and painstaking manner. Any one seeing the accuracy denoted by erasures and interlineations, and the marked evidences of the most exhaustive research, will value more than ever before, the legacy he has left us in his noble work. He was also something of a physician, for here are several books by him on epidemic diseases, bilious fevers, etc.

Here is a curious specimen of vegetable petrifaction, from Monroe Co., N. Y., which is a rock composed of a mass of leaves, many of them in perfect form.

We notice some shark's teeth, which were taken from green sand marl in New Jersey. Also specimens of silver ore, from the consolidated Virginia mine in Colorado, which has made monthly dividends of $1,080,000. This ore looks like hard, barren rock, not one thousandth part so attractive as the worthless rock near by, glittering with pyrites of iron.

Here are coils of iron, six inches square, which have been bent when cold, and iron bars tied in knots like a piece of cord; a piano whose case is made of wood from the famous old charter oak—and here is the oldest piano in America, made in Germany in 1745, an instrument of four and a half octaves, about seven feet long, and two and a half wide, the keys yellow with age, the legs turned neatly, and the case made of rosewood, or wood similar in appearance. Here is a skeleton of what is marked an extinct lizard, taken from the green marl in New Jersey. It would seem to have been designed for walking on two legs, and somewhat resembles a kangaroo. When in an upright position, the head must have been about fifteen feet above the ground. The length of the body is about twenty feet.

Did you ever hear of a whole forest of trees being turned into stone? Here is a piece of wood from a petrified forest in California, three miles long and one mile wide. It is supposed, that it was once flooded with water from a hot spring near by, which was impregnated with certain mineral properties, that produced this effect. We see also a piece of rock soap—a very soft, gritty stone, which will wear away when rubbed, and answers very well as a substitute for soap, when no better is to be had.

Here are magnificent displays of jewelry and silver ware, which are bewilderingly beautiful, and are constantly sur-

DIANA. (p. 14.)

rounded by crowds, anxious to get a glimpse of this enormous wealth. They do not have the opportunity every day to see a set of diamonds, necklace, coronet, earrings, and brooch, worth nearly $200,000, and cases filled with diamonds of lesser value, and all kinds of precious stones, beautifully set. We see the largest opal in the world,—oval in form, about three inches long, and two wide, which reflects the tints of the rainbow; it is wonderfully beautiful. It is worth $2,500.

The department of Great Britain and Ireland is very fine, but we can only notice some of the most interesting objects. Here are gorgeous tapestries of huge dimensions; exquisite lace and embroidered curtains; engravings and chromos; case after case of the best editions of standard works, which would warm the heart of a book lover; brass and silver musical instruments, which reflect like a mirror; guns and cutlery of the finest finish; cloths of all kinds, costly furs and robes, ladies' silk dresses and plain and figured velvets, of the richest material; shawls of almost every conceivable quality and pattern: and, in short, almost everything that necessity or luxury could require. Notice these furnished bedrooms, in the styles of Queen Anne, and India, respectively; so rich, and yet so quiet, the decorations and furniture so happily blended, as to make them look like the chambers of Peace.

Here is a splendid collection of cut glassware, which is a study for an artist. This goblet, so light and fragile that it makes one feel uncomfortable to take it up, and which is figured with a spirited design of St. George and the Dragon cut almost as delicately as a cameo, is worth $140. This pitcher, covered with mythological designs cut in the same exquisite manner, is priced at $250. These are cut by hand, and require the greatest skill and care on the part of the workman. There are hundreds of pieces of these costly articles, worth a fortune.

Here are extensive treasures in porcelain, which might be studied for days together, so rare are the designs and coloring. A plate, one of a set made for the Emperor of Germany, is like a beautiful picture. It is astonishing how such brilliant colors in such an elaborate picture can be burned on this material without the slightest blur or irregularity. This single plate is worth $60, which suggests the care and skill required in making them. A pair of vases not a foot in height, on the sides of which are representations of Landseer's famous dog pictures, "High and Low Life," colored in the same artistic manner, are priced at $1,000 each.

Here is an oak chest made of beams 660 years old, from Salisbury Cathedral, England, and carved with designs from Gothic architecture. The wood is of a rich, yellow color, is sound as ever, and would endure apparently for thousands of years. The chest represents a structure in the Gothic style and is an interesting study to lovers of the unique.

A CELEBRATED VASE FROM BRITISH MUSEUM. (p. 14.)

Here are samples of all sorts of tile for floors, wainscoting, panels, mantels, aud many other uses. The treasures of antiquity, the galleries of fine arts, the chivalric romance of the middle ages, all have been levied upon, to furnish designs for these beautiful decorations, intended to render homes more elegant, refined and artistic.

Under this canopy, is a life size statue of Thomas Carlyle. He is represented as seated in his easy arm chair, and his shaggy beard and mustache, which almost covers his face, his sunken cheeks, his wrinkled brow, his thoughtful, studious eyes, and his grim, defiant expression, all bear the impress of his stern independence, and his aggressive nature.

Let us examine these reproductions of ancient suits of armor, from the fifteenth and sixteenth centuries; the whole body cased in steel, except a small opening for the eyes, and the whole covered with elaborate designs. Here is one set, with ogre face on top of helmet; on the shield another, and other grotesque and hideous faces on elbows, knees, and breast, the remainder being filled up with rich tracery and carvings of dragons, unicorns, warlike scenes, and a profusion of strange, fantastic devices. As these suits are about the same size, it must be inferred that they represent the size of the average man, and if so, we must be larger than our ancestors, for I hardly think these suits could be put on by the average man of to-day.

Here is a very extensive collection of elegant *bric a brac,* with many reproductions of the art treasures in the museum at Kensington, London;—vases, shields, and table service of silver, chased with exquisite carvings—generally of spirited and fierce battle scenes. It is wonderful how our forefathers seemed to regard wars, and tournaments, as the first and greatest objects of life, judging from what they have left behind them.

Here is a most beautiful work of art, called "Milton's Shield," oval in form, about four feet long, and three feet wide, of silver, and covered with designs illustrating "Paradise Lost." In the centre we see Satan, in guise of a serpent, tempting our parents in Paradise. On the right, the archangel Michael, with spear and shield, hurling the lost spirits over the battlements of heaven; on the left, Satan encouraging his hosts to battle; and at the bottom, Michael, standing triumphant over Satan and his hosts: all of these, possessing artistic merit in the highest degree. This is valued at $8,000.

Another extraordinary work of art is called the "Helicon Vase," and represents the triumph of Music and Poetry.

Two large, reclining, antique figures are the most prominent features;—one representing Music with roll at her side and a pert cupid at her feet, looking up at her; the other representing Poetry, with harp and roll of manuscript before her,

THE FAMOUS WARWICK VASE. (p 14.)

while near is a spirited Pegasus. The piece is covered with the richest chasing, and beautiful designs appropriate to the subject. It is valued at $30,000.

But we must leave this attractive locality, with its thousands of other treasures which we cannot stop to notice, and will next visit

The French Department.

In this section we shall doubtless find many objects of great interest, for the French are a luxury loving people, and have an inborn love of the beautiful.

Their tapestries are celebrated throughout the world, and here we can see them and judge for ourselves.

Some of them are of immense size, about thirty by forty feet, and are covered with the most elaborate designs, in brilliant colors, and fully bear out all that we have heard of them. One of them is said to have three thousand different shades of color. Here is a large display of Pallissy ware, including vases, statues, and all sorts of parlor ornaments. Some of the pieces have fishes, foliage, fruits, flowers, and other figures, which look as if they were moulded and laid on, after the body of the piece was formed; so we may get some

idea of the wonderful skill required to make them. They
have rich, strong colors and a very bright lustre, and are exact
imitations of the work of the great originator,—Pallissy. You
remember the story of this wonderful man,—how he made
the discovery of this process the mission of his life, and through
long and weary years of poverty, and incessant toil night
and day, he braved the ridicule of his friends, and the taunts
of his family, and reduced himself nearly to beggary by his
experiments, until at last, he was rewarded with success, and
these costly articles are monuments of his unquenchable
energy and genius.

There are also beautiful vases of many different materials
and varieties, bronze statuary of great beauty, and clocks of
every description,—neat, handsome, unique, or fantastic.

Here are glossy velvets, shimmering satins, aristocratic
brocades, bewildering, plain and figured silks, and elegant
cashmere shawls of gorgeous coloring. There, we see dignified broadcloths, dressy cassimeres, jaunty plaids, and
numberless other varieties of wearing apparel. A book-
case of the style of Louis XV. is made of rich, dark wood,
most elaborately carved, and is valued at $5,000.

You would not suppose it possible for man to invent a machine to play on a piano, and yet some ingenious Frenchman
has done that very thing; and here it is, playing some of the
most difficult music, with as much precision and effect as an

FLORA. (p. 14.)

excellent pianist. It is constructed on pneumatic principles, and is worked by a crank. It is a case about four feet long, three feet high, and two feet wide, and is filled by bellows and complicated mechanism.

A folding book of pasteboard, perforated with holes corresponding to the notes of the music, is placed in the machine for every tune; and as these pass through, machinery is put in operation which causes artificial fingers to press the keys of the piano. The mechanism is very complicated, so that it is difficult to explain its workings in detail, but it seems to work to a charm.

We notice magnificent specimens of plate glass, about twelve by twenty-five feet in size, and as clear as crystal; ivory carving of the most ingenious description, wax and leather work, and an assortment of several kinds of carriages. Some of these have convex tire. They are elegant, and highly finished, but yet in gracefulness of design, and completeness of finish, they are not equal to many, exhibited by makers in our own country.

Before leaving this department, let us notice this curious Gobelin tapestry, dating back by tradition to the year 1615. It is worked by hand, in worsted; and although in places faded, and disfigured by age, it still shows traces of its former beauty. The subject is the birth of Christ; the babe in the manger, the mother of Christ, the wise men bringing their gifts with expressions of adoration; the cherubs above,—all are finely brought out. It was brought from Europe by a French nobleman, and, in 1792, was in St. Augustine's chapel, Montreal.

The Swiss watches are famous throughout the world, and here is a good opportunity to see some of the best. It is a wonder how so much complicated mechanism, requiring such absolute perfection of movement, can be contained in the space of a watch. Here, for instance, is a gentleman's watch of ordinary size. It is a stem winder, and repeats the minutes, hours, and quarters of an hour. It has double concentric time, and will show the hour at Chicago and New York, or any two places, and has a perpetual calendar showing the months, days of month and week, and phases of the moon. The price of this is $1,150. We notice a lady's watch, about an inch in diameter, which will strike the hours and quarters of an hour,—price $1,200. But here is the smallest watch in the world, set in the head of a pencil case, and less than half an inch in diameter. Another is set in a ring, and does not make a clumsy setting, either. Here are music-boxes, which make music like that of an infant orchestra, and one is contained in a small Swiss chalet, on the top of which sits a little bird, with brilliant plumage, which, at certain parts of the music, turns its head, flutters its tail in the most natural manner, and pours forth a song which is a

ANTIQUE EGYPTIAN VASE.

wonderful imitation of the trills and warbles of a song bird.

There is a clock also, which, when it strikes, folding doors open, two miniature trumpeters appear with their trumpets and play a duet, each a different part, in perfect time and unison. At the close of the music, the figures withdraw and the doors close. The price of this is $160.

We will next visit Russia, and here is a genuine surprise, for most of us have supposed this nation far behind others in manufactures, and the fine arts, and yet we see excellent school-apparatus, books, maps, the finest cutlery, satins, laces, velvets, brocades, and other fabrics of choicest color and texture, rich display of furs, statuary, carving in gold and silver, porcelain, silver plate, and embroidery in gold and silver,— all evincing the most consummate skill and exquisite taste. Here is a work of marvelous beauty in silver and gold. It represents a silk handkerchief with elegant colored border, thrown across a golden basket or server,—the imitation of the glistening silk being exquisite beyond description. A sleigh scene moulded in silver, is a very spirited design,—three horses, graceful and fleet, and at their utmost speed, are drawing a sleigh with two occupants. Another article of wonderful beauty, is a malachite table, the top resting on gilt standard. This kind of marble is green, figured and grained with black. The top of the table is made by fitting together

different pieces, selected for their beauty, and joined so perfectly, that the joints are hardly discernable. In the middle is
fitted a piece like a star, and around it a circle of patterns
mottled like shell work, making a most charming combination of colors and designs. A mantel of the same material,
is a perfect gem of the kind, and is priced at $540. Another
exquisite piece of work is a gilt clock for mantel-piece, on
which a falconer is seated on a spirited charger with bow in
case, and arrow in quiver. The hunter has reined up his steed,
and the falcon rests on his outstretched hand, with wings
outspread, and looking intently forward to discern the prey.
Here is a water pitcher, with groups of statuary on four sides,
all in silver, and exhibiting the most astonishing skill and
workmanship. In fact, wherever we go a surprise awaits us,
at the richness and beauty of the articles which meet our
eyes.

In the German department we find extensive collections of
books,—the fine editions of standard authors, school-books,
maps, charts and chromos, some of which are very fine.
There are also clocks of many antique and ornamental designs, and tapestries of large size and great richness. There
is a model of the Hamburgh steamers which represents one
cut in two, lengthwise, and shows exactly the internal construction. There are many other interesting articles here,
but it seems as if the display in this department is not quite

CASE OF FINE FIGURED SILKS. (p. 80.)

as complete as might be expected from such a great power as Germany, and not so good as the displays she makes in some of the other buildings.

We will pass to Austria and Hungary, and we see here a very extensive display of delicate, green, cut-glass, and near it an equally varied collection of the finest Bohemian glassware. We are shown a goblet which was made several weeks ago by a new process just discovered. It reflects the most brilliant colors, and is thought to be an important discovery, as its cost is comparatively moderate. Among other objects worthy of note is a magnificent vase of cut glass, of large size and elaborate workmanship, worth $640; an immense collection of costly pipes and an extremely fine display of jewelry.

In the Belgium department we see laces, silks, tapestry, fire arms, musical instruments, linen goods, blankets, inlaid wood-work, sewing machines, clothes, glassware, and a beautiful carved oak fire place, all showing the varied industries of the country, and the skill of her artisans.

In the Netherlands we see fine assortments of soaps, glassware, blankets, marbles, tapestries, and beautiful lacquer-work. A Bengalese loom is shown, which is of extremely rude construction, and made of a few pieces of rough wood, and yet it has in it, a piece of cloth of neat pattern and colors. On a large lacquered screen, there are lovely pictures, inlaid with mother of pearl, and some of the designs are:—

Scenes from Goethe.

It is one of the most exquisite works of art in the whole
building.   The designs are about a foot square, and four of
them are from Goethe's "Faust."   The first represents Faust
in his alchemist's study, a stately old man, with fine face, and
long, gray beard, standing by the open casement longing to
discover the elixir of life, and so renew his youth,—leaning on
his hand, a flood of morning sunlight streaming through, and
resting on his laboratory, and gilding crucible, retort, and
chemical apparatus with gorgeous hues.

Mephistopheles appears to Faust, and offers him youth and
beauty for his soul; he accepts, and is transformed to a
beautiful young man, meets, and afterward wins, and ruins the
fair Marguerite; and the next scene represents the poor, peni-
tent Marguerite, about to enter the church, dressed in rich
silk, her dress, the door lintel, and the steps, illumined by
golden sunlight.   Back in the shadow of the church stands
Faust, watching her enter, his fine face shrouded in sadness,
as if reproaching himself; while Mephistophles, the fiend in
human shape, dressed in red robes, and large plumed hat,

stands back, his sharp, demonaic face wearing a smile of exultation at the ruin he has wrought.

The next scene represents Marguerite in the church, touching the holy water near the door; her face serious and thoughtful. The worshippers are in the distance, but she shrinks back as if unworthy to join them, while an inquisitive old man looks back at her, as if curious to know her history. The glorious sunlight streams through a window, and floods her with its radiance, as if to disperse the gloom and sorrow from her mind.

The next scene depicts her in the church-yard, prostrate at her mother's tomb, her hands clasped in sorrow and remorse, her golden hair streaming down; while at a distance the village gossips have gathered around the public pump, and she is evidently the subject of their tattle, for they are looking and pointing sneeringly towards her. In the back ground are seen the quaint old houses, with their ancient gables, and the venerable old church, sombre and imposing in its shadows.

Remember, that every part of these elaborate pictures,— sunlight and shadow,—the expression of features, and the elegant costumes,—are made by pieces of mother of pearl, inlaid together so marvellously perfect, as to produce these wonderful effects. This beautiful piece of work is valued at $900.

Let us next visit the colonies of Great Britain,—and first we will pay our respects to Canada, as she has by far the most extensive array, and has evidently intended to show what she can do. This department is intensely practical, and is designed to show the material resources of the country: and so we see all kinds of saws, leather, stoves, boots and shoes, harness, nails, tacks, copper, tin, horse shoes made by machinery, spikes, carpenter's tools, furs, farming implements, organs, sewing machines, fire extinguishers, pottery, rope, woolen goods, safes, billiard tables, soaps, crackers, marble, slate, granite, and a model of one of their public school buildings, built of brick on the modern style, high, well ventilated rooms, and the latest improvements in seats, desks, and blackboards. Here is a column of coal, twelve feet high, representing the thickness of the coal bed. One would get the impression surely, that Canada was a wide awake country, full of brain and sinew.

Suppose we call next on South Australia. Here we see many specimens of marble, an extensive collection of copper and silver ores, wool, a magnificent display of native woods, wheat, barley, wines, preserved beef, furs, leather, and tin ore. Queensland is a part of Australia, but has a separate department. We find a splendid collection of woods, jute leather, candied fruits, wheat, wool, cocoons, coal, books, tobacco, tin, and fine specimens of gold in nuggets, in the quartz rock.   There are also samples of Malachite marble, and copper ores.   What a wealth of resources do these articles represent, and yet these are but a tithe of what she has contributed towards the world's wealth.   Here is an illustration of the old adage,

All's not Gold that Glitters,

for we see a column that looks like that precious metal, three feet square at the base, about eighteen feet high, and sixteen inches square at the top, which is the size of the actual amount of gold exported from Queensland, from 1868 to 1875.   Would you believe that it weighs $65\frac{1}{2}$ tons, and was worth $35,000,-000.   A very nice nugget for a small place to present to the world's business uses.

The best showing that New South Wales makes, is a column representing the gold exported from that colony from 1851 to 1874, which is about seven feet square from bottom to top, and about eleven feet high, and was worth $167,949,-355.   Who says the world is not getting rich ?

British Columbia proudly exhibits a pyramid about six feet square at base, running to a point about nine feet high, representing the gold exported from 1858 to 1875.

And New Zealand has the enviable distinction of showing a column four and a half feet square and twenty-three feet and five inches high, which represents the gold she exported from 1862 to 1875. It weighs 246 tons and is worth $151.271,293. Let our wise heads establish our currency on a gold basis,—who cares, if we only had these big nuggets safely stowed away in Uncle Sam's pockets.

By the side of this dazzling representation of wealth, New Zealand condescends to exhibit samples of jute, wool, native woods, leather, rope, mats, coal, and a collection of hatchets, spears, and other articles of very curious workmanship, made by the natives. There is also shown a hideous figure-head, for a native water craft,—which is a rough image painted red with sharp nose, body made of a carved board, and large claws, probably made to frighten their foes, and admirably adapted for that purpose.

Amongst the Jamaica exhibits, we notice a large collection of fine sea shells and coral rock, beautiful inlaid tables, native woods of great richness and variety, wool, lace work, and sugar.

The Bahamas have contributed specimens of very elaborate straw and shell work, flower stands, immense sea shells, sponges, and a fine collection of native woods.

From the Gold Coast of Africa, has come an interesting collection of articles that throw much light on the condition and manner of life of the native African.   Here are matted baskets, and colored cloth, which is surprisingly good for savages to weave; matting of red, black and blue colors; their calabashes and cooking vessels, some of them tolerably well made; idols, rudely carved in wood, whose distinguishing features are their big heads, and dwarfish bodies,—and a rude harp of the most primitive pattern.

We find in the section allotted to Cape of Good Hope, wines, wool, ostrich plumes, native woods, cotton and wheat, all excellent samples.   A young stuffed ostrich, two days old, is as large as a half grown goose, and another, fourteen days old is as large as a medium sized turkey.   Here are sets of jewelry, made by natives, of musk melon seed, and a woman's, head dress, made of a band covered with teeth.

Tasmania exhibits wool, very rich furs, tin and tin ore, slate, coal, native woods, and wheat that looks like wax, so clear and transparent is the berry.

We will now visit the section of one of the most wonderful countries on the globe, whose history and literature are shrouded in the mists of antiquity, whose people are an enigma and paradox,—a land of fabulous wealth, of Oriental magnificence, of great intellectual acuteness, whose past is a romance, and whose present is a mystery,—I mean India.   Here is a set of furniture from Bombay, carved in black wood; and we see the most elaborate carving of storks, turtles, alligators, and curious devices of all kinds. Also a collection of their musical instruments,—a large bass horn, a two stringed affair something like a banjo, a kettle drum, and a sort of clarionet, all very neatly made. Here we behold one of their famous Cashmere shawls woven by hand, which is valued at $1,155. Here are elegant pieces of tapestry, beautiful inlaid marble vases, and silver table service, all of which display the wonderful ingenuity and artistic tastes of this people; and yet, look at this plow and contrast it with these elegant articles of luxury. It is one of their native plows, and is made of a rough log with a bend in it, having a rod of iron like a crowbar, projecting in front to scratch the ground, a rough crooked beam and a small stick projecting backwards for a handle, and a rude yoke made to tie to the front of the oxen's heads. Look at that, and then at this magnificent embroidery of woolen and gold, which dreams of Oriental splendor cannot surpass; and no wonder we are amazed at the contrast.

We see specimens of their sculptured slabs, the same as cover the sides of their immense temples. They are not of the finest finish, and resemble the designs on the Assyrian marbles. There is also a collection of photographic views of their temples, and some of those wonderful edifices must be nearly two hundred feet high, and about one hundred and fifty feet square at the base, but diminishing in size towards the top. The sides are covered from top to bottom with designs of elephants, lions, idols, chariots and warriors—a perfect labyrinth of ornamentation, aud portrayals of historical events, while the top is crowned by immense figures and domes. The ceilings inside are decorated with circular designs, and the sides with a wilderness of columns or pilasters, covered with carving from base to ceiling. Some of the temples are built with colums of great height, above which are cornices and friezes of the richest character.

Here are water vessels, swords, guns and spears of fine workmanship, many of them ornamented in the most artistic manner. We find also Hindoo prayers, which look like a few irregular marks, printed on illuminated sheets of brilliant colors, and all done by hand. There are paintings on mica, brought from the Indian Museum at London, which represent the Hindoo Deities, and which are extremely singular and grotesque, but the colors are of wonderful brilliancy and clearness. From Ceylon has come a perfect figure of an elephant, carved by a native out of a piece of plumbago.

We will next notice the Brazilian section, and we see an excellent display of the country's resources. In our childish days, a picture in our geography, representing the Brazilian diamond mines, in which a long row of unfortunate black men were kept hard at work looking for the precious treasures, while near by stood the overseer, lash in hand, invested the subject with peculiar interest. Here we see some of the

famous gems, of different sizes, shapes, and degrees of purity.
The largest and most perfect diamond, which is perhaps about
half an inch square, is worth $13,000, and there are a large
collection of many other precious stones. Here are samples
of coal, iron ore, crystals, furs, leather, silk, soap, furniture,
hats, shoes, cotton goods, earthenware, wickerwork, embroidery, books, including books for the blind, inlaid wood-work,
maps, charts and engravings. A case of stuffed Brazilian
birds and of flowers and butterflies is a marvel of beauty, and
is fairly radiant with rich, tropical hues. The books and exquisite crayon sketches are indicative of cultivated and refined
tastes. A department is here, showing an artisans school,
which is decorated by an inscription, stating that it is for
boys from twelve to fifteen years of age, to make them "clean
artisans." On one side is a motto from Blair, "He who
knows not what it is to labor, knows not what it is to enjoy;"
and on the other, one from Shakespeare:

> "To business that we love, we rise betime,
> And go to it with delight."

There are models and drawings of machinery of many kinds,
and of bridges, lockgates and other public works, with charts,
working tools, drawing instruments, and other appurtenances
needful for such an institution.

Suppose we now take a glance at Mexico. We see here an
immense meteoric mass, weighing two tons, which looks

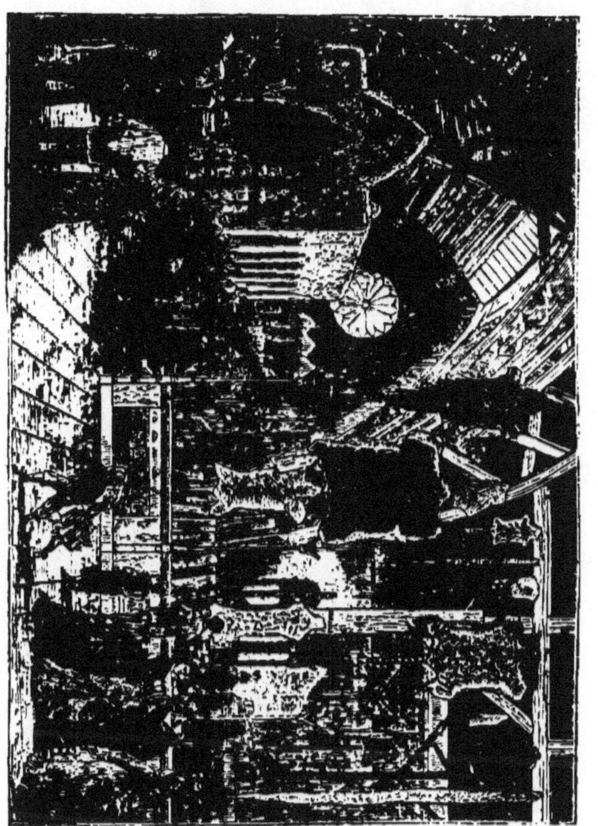

VIEW IN BRAZILIAN DEPARTMENT.

almost like pure iron, red and rusty from exposure. It is not very comforting to think of these ugly lumps of iron, whizzing around our earth, and every now and then, one descending upon it with the velocity of a cannon ball.

Here is a species of rock which looks exactly like hard coal tar, the same as roofers use. It seems to be very hard and tough, and formerly the Mexicans used to make their weapons out of it.

Let us notice the slabs of Mexican onyx, which are of surpassing beauty. The combination of colors and shades is wonderful; some parts look like fine boxwood, others like lignum-vitae wood; others are dappled with green tints and cloudy shades, in the most exquisite manner, and look like mother of pearl.

A table whose top is of this material, is indescribably beautiful, and is a study, as much as a fine picture, or masterpiece of art. The richness of the Mexican silver mines is illustrated by an exhibit of a solid button of this metal, about seven feet in diameter, and ten inches thick, which is worth $72,000. We notice choice books in elegant, morocco bindings, and fine engravings, which indicate that the Mexicans have a knowledge of the art preservative.

Let us next go over to the Spanish section, which is on the main aisle of the buildings and has an imposing front about thirty feet in height, which suggests something of the former glory of this once powerful nation.

On the upper part is a picture of the Spanish crown and coat of arms, while above, is another of a figure representing Spain, drawing back a curtain, behind which is seen America rising from the sea in the far distance. On one side of this is the portrait of Isabella, on the other of Columbus; and at one end is a portait of Pizarro, the famous conqueror of Peru, clad in armor—a fine looking military face, full beard and mustache, large, cold, blue eyes, aquiline nose, and haughty bearing; at the other is the portrait of De Soto, the ill-fated discoverer of the Mississippi, a fine face, with grey hair, beard and mustache.

In another place is the portrait of Cortez, the cruel conqueror; a well-favored face with large eyes, regular features and full beard and mustache; and also that of Ponce De Leon, a kingly head and figure, a grand face, black hair and beard slightly sprinkled with grey: he looks like a natural leader of men, and such a leader as brave men would delight to follow. In this department, we notice pieces of royal armor,—helmet and breastplate embossed with battle scenes, lines of cannon, masses of troops, and fierce conflicts man to man, all of which are wonderfully spirited studies. Here is an immense block of copper ore; fine specimens of iron and lead ores; coal, and petrified wood, the bark

still retaining its natural appearance. There are collections
of porcelain and glassware, a beautiful silver platter valued
at $2,000, highly finished swords, brasswork, tile, elegant
silks, brocades with the richest figuring, delicate laces,
handsome shawls and tapestries, a large assortment of
wearing apparel, fancy woolen blankets, rich figured curtains,
fans, and samples of beautiful marbles. A handsome young
Spaniard seems to have charge of this section, such a youth
as Ponce De Leon must have been when a young man, tall,
graceful, erect, a fine head, fresh, handsome face, and a dignified bearing. Portugal has a very handsome display of jewelry and silver work, shawls and embroidery, rich silks and
figured velvets.

We will next turn our attention to Turkey and introduce
our observations by a description of

The Pretty Turk.

What means this throng which blocks up the aisle, and seems
to be drawn irresistibly to a common center? There is nothing
that attracts more eyes than a pretty young lady, and particularly, when that young lady is a Turkish belle. Notice
how the proud and accomplished city beauty turns aside, as if
accidentally, to see the attractive stranger; while the ingenu-

ous country girl, looks as if she beheld an apparition, and
drinks in at one long glance, her dress, features, expression,
and general deportment. A graceful, *petite* figure, a well-
shaped head, and finely arched neck, a *pose* that would befit
a queen, large lustrous black eyes, eyebrows that look as if
penciled in India ink, an aquiline nose, a pretty mouth, a
fair complexion, and hair black as night, and dressed in the
most approved modern style. Her acquaintance with our institutions, has been sufficient to induce her to adopt a light,
graceful costume, quite in harmony with the slight dash of
natural coquetry which she cannot repress.

The swarthy young Turks, with their immense turbans,
baggy trousers, and highly colored jackets, crowd about her
and she greets them with hearty *bon hommie.*

The old Turk, with a suspicious red nose, and a deplorable
lack of familiarity with the English language, and who has
charge of cases of rare old coins near by, jabbers in vain to
catch customers. His *confrére*, who is endeavoring to turn
an honest penny, by the sale of rich coffee colored pipes, and
tobacco that is redolent of honey, invites attention to his
wares in vain. The charming young lady has the field, and
captures the crowd.

In a case near by are some scimaters, swords and spears,
which look as if they had done service on bloody battle-fields
centuries ago. And here is a collection of old coins, some of

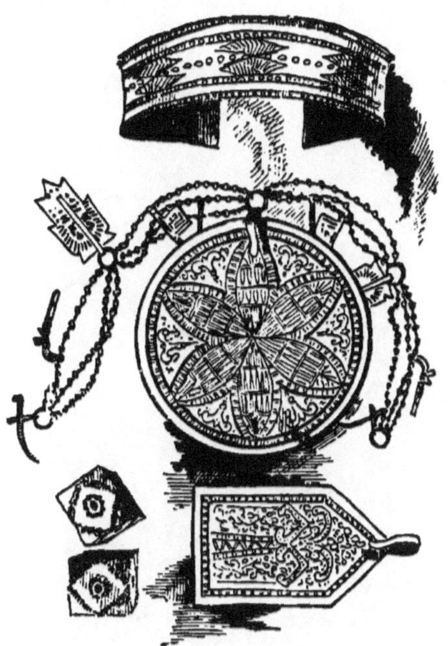

SILVER FILIGREE WORK. (p. 60.)

silver, stamped with the heads of Assyrian kings, long before the days of the prophets, and look like those seen in drawings of the Assyrian marbles. Others, bearing the image of Julius Cæsar; others, those of Egyptian kings, in the dim, remote past; and others, the figures of Roman centurions. There are pieces of silver, bearing cabalistic marks upon them, which none but a learned antiquarian could decipher; pieces of brass, with marks quite illegible, all battered and smoothed by century after century of use. If they could only speak, what mysteries of the past could they unfold; what glimpses they could give of forgotten peoples, and extinct civilizations! Here are swords, battle axes, shields and helmets which are covered with ancient designs, and which centuries ago, were used on bloody fields of carnage. Here are muskets, pistols and swords, glittering with the most lavish ornamentation of inlaid work of silver and mother of pearl.

Here is a harp, which, the Turks insist, is an exact copy of the harp of David. They have other harps, richer in design, but this style, they claim, has been transmitted from age to age, since the time of David, and can be traced back through the dim centuries. It is a plainly constructed instrument of black wood about three feet high, and twenty inches wide at the base, and has about one hundred strings, seemingly of about the same material as catgut violin strings. We are shown articles of furniture, toys and mementos, purporting to be cut and carved from Abraham's oak, and olive wood from the Mount of Olives. If you regard the Turks as a semi-barbarous people, with little or no knowledge of the arts and manufactures, you are greatly mistaken; for here are beautiful specimens of household furniture, richly carved and superbly finished. Here also, are books which are finely bound and illustrated; rich tapestries and woven goods, that are much better than our general impression of Turkish civilization would lead us to expect. The household utensils shown here, indicate a people not unmindful of the comforts of life; and the carpenters' tools resemble ours somewhat, though ruder and in many respects much inferior.

We will now go over to Italy, and here we find an atmosphere of art and beauty. It would require hours to describe the exquisite marble, bronze and terra cotta statuary, the wonderful carving in black walnut and ebony, the latter often inlaid with pearl—centre tables inlaid with marvellous skill, the top of one resting on the stooping body of a negro carved in ebony,—jewelry, porcelain, cameos, silver filagree work, specimens of mosaic, ancient armor, books, velvets, and a table in mosaic worth $1,500. Here is a violin 171 years old, that was used by Pagininni, valued at $1,000. It looks old and dirty, and not worth more than $2.50. Notice this beautiful table on which is the "Cathedral of Milan" inlaid in mother of pearl, with its wonderful imitation of sunlight; also this

THE GREENLAND METEORITE.

table and settee carved in stone, which are covered by a maze of elaborate designs of game, guns, fruit, &c., of exquisite beauty; and hundreds of other articles, which show the wonderful ingenuity and artistic taste of this people.

Reluctantly we leave sunny Italy, and turn to snowy Norway. Here are iron and nickel ores, two-wheeled vehicles much like our sulkies, sledges of fine construction, and handsomely painted and varnished; a skillfully carved bedstead and sideboard, and furs of black and polar bears. This is the land of the fierce and adventurous Norsemen, who were the terror of the seas, and adjacent countries, more than a thousand years ago, and here is a display of very old weapons, either the same, or similar to those used by them. Among them is a cross-bow of steel about two feet long, that must have required great strength to draw it, an old musket inlaid with pearl, having a flint lock, which turns with a crank,—ancient battle axes with carved handles, immense swords seemingly for both hands, the blades about five feet long, and the handles one foot in length,—one with blade cerrated. There are also books, rope, cloths, oils, porcelain and glassware, upright pianos, rather small but well finished, filigree silver jewelry, and wax figures showing the features and costume of a Laplander. He is dressed in a blue coat embroidered with red and yellow, a cap with an arrangement on the top which looks like a small pillow, green stockings and moccasins, and heavy fur gloves. He has long coarse hair, sunken eyes, broad cheek bones, large mouth, and by no stretch of the imagination could be called handsome.

From Sweden we notice fine porcelain, glass and earthen ware, magnificent vases, terra cotta work, cutlery, wall paper, fine cloths and furs, all kinds of tools, a splendid display of iron ores, nails, iron castings and car wheels. An object that attracts much notice, is an immense stuffed stag, about nine feet in length. He has been brought down upon his knees, by a rifle ball in his side; while standing by looking at him, are two Swedish men and a woman, life-size figures in wax,— one of the men holding a rifle. The group are remarkably life like in appearance, and the position of the noble old stag is so natural, that you involuntarily pity him in his dying agony.

Here is a meteorite from Greenland, weighing over six tons, which looks like a mass of copper ore, and is said to belong to the tertiary formation, which relates back to a time, untold ages before man inhabited the earth. It is valued at $7,000.

Sweden was once a formidable warlike power, and for a long time had much to do in making the history of Europe. We see here a wax figure showing the uniform of her soldiers in 1632, in the time of Gustavus Adolphus II. The uniform consists of a helmet of steel, a large white linen collar, broad leather sword belt, blue sash, heavy metal breastplate, buck-

A Deer Made of Spikes, and a Curious Ethnological Ornament in
Swedish Department.

skin gloves and girdle, blue breeches and stockings, heavy low shoes, and the weapons were a spear, and a battle axe having a blade on each side. Here is an Esquimaux canoe made of skins, about twenty feet long, and eighteen inches wide on top, sharply pointed at each end, and very lightly but strongly constructed. There is a hole in the middle large enough to admit the body of the occupant, who sits in the bottom of the boat, and wears a garment which is fastened water tight around the opening in the boat. A little frame in front supports his harpoon and coil of hide, his spear is by his side, and he is provided with a short oar with paddle at each end. Every part of it is so light, that a man could easily shoulder the whole outfit, and yet it is strong enough to ride upon the roughest seas.

We will now turn our steps to old Egypt,—the cradle of our race, whose past is o'ershadowed with the dim mists of antiquity. Wonderful to say, this fossilized country has actually possessed the enterprise to build a stately front on the main aisle of the building, something like the Spanish, which is suggestive, in the color of its decorations, and the style of its construction, of the old Egyptian civilization, which flourished in the infancy of the world. On this front are painted these cheery and neighborly words,

"The oldest people of the world sends its morning greeting to the youngest nation."

In return for this courteous salutation, we hope the Exposition may be the means of infusing some of the enterprise, and intelligence of this western world, into the benumbed system of our venerable neighbor. It is not strange, that in this new country, we have a passion for something antiquated; we have wealth, luxury, refinement, the arts, architectural excellence, fine cities, elegant homes, and spacious temples, but we have not *age*, and so we have naturally a craving to see the old, old relics and vestiges of ages and peoples which flourished thousands of years ago. We see here a model of the largest pyramid, situated near Cairo, built 4,000 years B.C., which gives a clear conception of the magnitude of those massive structures. The pyramid is 470 feet in height, covering about thirteen acres. The model is about two feet square, in height about the same, and is covered by steps about one-eighth of an inch in height from base to summit. The real steps on the pyramid are described by travelers as nearly breast high to an ordinary man, and the same in width. And here we see a bust of the builder; the man who could command one hundred thousand poor, toiling subjects, to spend their weary lives in erecting this senseless pile, a monument both of his despotic power, and supreme folly. The bust shows a pleasing face, regular features, a small head and body, with square shoulders, and a physique very much unlike the beef-eating Briton, and beer loving Teuton of these latter days.

Here are old silver ornaments, bracelets for the wrists, arms

TUNISIAN FABRICS AND EMBROIDERY. (p. 78.)

and ankles, about two inches wide, and perhaps worn by the
Egyptian belles, before the decalogue was given to man,
amid the thunders of Sinai. There is a complete photographed copy of the Koran here, about an inch and a half in length,
an inch wide, and half an inch thick; but it requires a magnifying glass to read it.

Here, also, we see the bust of an Ethiopian queen, who
lived 900 years B. C. The type of features seems to resemble
the Egyptian very strongly, the same flat eyes, high, arched
brows, broad nose, thick lips, and oval face, but yet the features are beautiful, and the expression pleasing. We see an
old Arabic door, made of ebony and ivory; and belonging to
a mosque of the fourteenth century. It is covered with irregular, carved blocks of ivory; and has the appearance of great
age. It is very small for a work of such elaborate finish, being only about two and a half feet wide, and six feet high.
We see here excellent specimens of maps, lithographs, engravings, and books.

In the Bible, the wild boar is alluded to as one of the fiercest of beasts; and these tusks are most convincing proofs of
that fact; for they are at least six inches long, and an inch and
a half broad, and have a most savage look about them.

Here is a tusk of that terrible animal the hippopotamus;
which is about sixteen inches long, and three inches in diam-

eter at the base; and which is quite strong enough to thrust into a tree, as he is said to do when angry.

This fine, reddish colored cloth, is woven from the bark of the wild fig tree.

In Egypt, the camel and dromedaries are as great a convenience as the railroad trains are with us; and here we see their saddles, embroidered with gilt lace, and looking very comfortable and inviting. These slabs of rough boulders, which are about two feet long, and one foot wide, and are carved like the ornamental border of a page filled with Arabic characters, are grave-stones from Abyssinia.

The Egyptians have from time immemorial, been lovers of luxury and splendor, and the passion lingers yet, for here we see a table cover, magnificently embroidered with gold, worth $4,000; and a jacket, and mantle, of exquisite richness, ornamented with feathers from peacocks, and other birds of brilliant plumage, which would entirely throw into the shade, any costume ever dreamed of on our shores.

For my part, I never expected to gaze upon the features of that Pharaoh who so vexed Moses, and the children of Israel, by his inconstant pranks, about 1,350 years B. C.; but here he is represented by this bust, the original of which was found in Egypt. He is shown as a young man, and however hard his heart may have been, he certainly had a most engaging countenance, if this is a correct likeness. The face

TUNISIAN JUGS, VASES, CUPS AND DRUM. (p. 76.)

is oval and regular, the eyes slightly flattened, the nose large, and the mouth and chin small and delicate. The bust represents a large person, and is probably larger than life size; the upper part of the head is high, signifying a large brain, and a head-dress is worn, which is ornamented in front with figures of serpents.

Such are some of the most remarkable objects in this interesting department, which are suggestive of the dim past, and lure the mind and imagination back to dynasties, and civilizations, long since forgotten.

Not very far from this, we find the section allotted to Tunis, and here we perceive an object of rare interest. It is a part of the pavement of a temple in Carthage, dedicated to Diana. This fragment is about ten feet long, and seven feet high, and is but a very small portion of a once spacious floor, but such was its brittleness, owing to its extreme age, that only this perfect specimen could be taken up. It represents a huge, fierce lion, with tail lashing with fury, glaring eyes, and defiant attitude; the body of a dull purple color, the eyes black, and the mane of a reddish shade. All this is made by thousands of stones of different colors, about half an inch square, which are laid in Mosaic, and closely fitted together. A critic says of it, that "the boldness of design, and the wonderful attitude and coloring, assign to it the most flourishing period of Carthage;" and it suggests the extraordinary wealth and splendor of those ancient powers, when such exquisite work as this was made to be trodden upon on the floors of their temples.

Near this are some farming implements, which show that those remains of former grandeur, do not inspire much enterprise in the men who vegetate about them; for here we see a rake made of rough pieces of wood fastened together; a pitchfork, which is merely a forked sapling, with the bark taken off; a plow made of a crooked bough of a tree, with sharp, iron point in front to scratch the ground, and a small handle to hold it; a shovel, which is but a wooden blade, fastened to a stick; and a threshing machine, resembling a stone boat, with a few slats of iron stuck in the bottom, on the front and sides, with rows of flints set in between. This is drawn over the scattered grain by oxen, and bruises it until the kernels are separated. The Bey of Tunis has sent a case of weapons, muskets, swords, and pistols, finely finished and inlaid with silver and pearls. There are also very brilliant silks, and gold embroidery on caps, slippers, jackets, and belts. In a show case, there is a richly chased silver table service, and a collection of old battle axes, helmets, shields, swords, cimeters, and spears, which look as if they were used centuries ago.

Suppose we now take a walk through the Chinese department. This is one of the most crowded places in the build-

VIEW IN CHINESE DEPARTMENT.

ing, so interesting and brilliant are the objects exhibited. For instance here is a screen, the frame of which is made of richly carved black wood,—the inside being of colored silk on which is painted quaint designs of birds, with wonderfully long tails,—queer looking shrubs and flowers all in the most gorgeous coloring; or see those pictures of warlike and fanciful scenes in lacquer work; or those large and beautiful porcelain vases of such delicate coloring; or these pieces of exquisite embroidery on colored silk, and shawls; or this magnificent parlor-set in black wood, artistically carved, and upholstered with the richest figured green silk, making it fit for the palace of a Crœsus; or these stately figured brocades, and exquisite white fans covered with birds and flowers in rapturous colors, delicate enough for a fairy to flutter. Wherever we go, there is a maze of this wonderful lacquer work, of painting on silk and screens, curious carving, fantastic designs on porcelain, and rich furniture. But one of the most appalling pieces of work, is a carved bedstead, which took fifteen men three years to finish,—equal to one long life of constant labor. It has a canopy of wood over it, on each side of which, are two battle scenes, the figures carved out of wood; under the cornice, is a wide fringe of wood, perhaps sixteen inches wide, made of hard wood boards about an inch and a quarter thick, and these are throughout a mass of the most elaborate carving of small designs of birds, foliage, fruits, and flowers; so that when you see the objects in the foreground, you can discern others still further back, making a complete mass of the most intricate work. Then below these, are four groups of figures at the corners, each one a study by itself, and making nearly the whole surface a mass of carving. This is valued at $4,000; not a high price for forty-five years steady work, requiring such skillful labor, and artistic taste.

Another wonderful piece of carving, is an ivory ship, with a large company on the deck, and in the cabin, engaged in different amusements and occupations, the work looking as if the whole were carved from a solid piece of ivory.

The Japanese section is somewhat similar to the Chinese. Here, too, we see carving, lacquer work, painting on silk, a bedstead of black wood, the foot carved with figures of fishes, and turtles, and the head with a marine view of rocks, shells, moss and turtles.

There is in that case, a rock crystal about seven inches in diameter, which looks like a solid piece of the purest glass, and reflects everything upside down.

Here is a funny picture designed by some Japanese Landseer, and painted on silk in the richest colors. It represents a procession of foxes dressed as men, in gay attire, and walking on their hind legs; some bearing merchandise, standards, and palanquins, and having all the airs and importance of a company of dandies.

CHINESE SCREENS AND INLAID LACQUER WORK. (p. 79.)

We notice embroidery on silk, pictures on leather, and exquisite screens, adorned with pictures of birds of gorgeous plumage, all having the most brilliant combination of colors; also, wonderful carving, and medallions in ivory with porcelain, covered with the most delicate designs; a shallow bowl of this ware, about four feet in diameter, is covered with a mass of fanciful figuring of birds, foliage and flowers, and is priced at $300; immense vases, about ten feet high are valued at $2,500 each. Horses are used but little in Japan, so that most of their traveling carriages are drawn by hand. Here are some of them, which look very much like large baby-wagons. They have boxes about four feet long, are on springs, are covered, and wide enough for one person to sit in easily, and give one an impression of comfort. Persons from Japan say, that the men who make it a business to draw these vehicles, are nearly as swift as horses, some have drawn them seventy miles a day; but their roads are as hard and smooth as a floor. Here are gongs that look something like a banjo, and a musical instrument made of richly carved ebony and ivory, which has thirteen strings, and a sounding board about seven feet long. Here is a Chinese weapon, supposed to be three thousand years old, made of brass, the handle plain, and the blade about three feet long, looking like a large carving knife.

Here are books, engravings, surgical instruments, and cutlery, and waxwork, life size, which is extremely good, and is an accurate copy of the form and complexion of the Japanese. There is also iron armor, the cap also of iron, with a wide lap extending down on the shoulders, and looking like a sailor's oil-skin cap.

The little kingdom of the Sandwich Islands has an interesting section, in which we see a case of articles sent by Queen Emma. In it are large circular wooden boxes, highly polished, plumes of gaily colored feathers, calabashes, an old pipe, which looks as if it had descended from former generations, and a cape made of black, yellow, and red feathers, woven in a fabric. Here are beautiful specimens of coral,—of lava from volcanoes,—a stalk of sugar cane twenty-six feet in length; and a model of a native brig made without nails, but fastened together with thongs, the bottom, ends, and sides being separate pieces, and the sails made of matting.

A necklace is shown which was made by braiding about fifty human hairs together in a cord, no larger than small wire, done in the neatest manner imaginable, and as there is a large coil of this, it must have been a work of infinite patience and labor. Here is a queer cloak worn by bird catchers, which is made by tying bunches of long grass to netting, one tuft overlapping another, making a thatched covering.

We see a very handsome table, inlaid with native many-colored woods; cases of stuffed birds, of red, green, and yel-

CURIOUS CHINESE CARVED FURNITURE. (p. 79.)

low plumage; and samples of rice, sugar, jute, and other articles of production. The very intelligent gentleman in charge informs us, that the population is but fifty or sixty thousand, and constantly decreasing; that a good system of schools is established, and that the country is becoming more and more civilized, according to our standard, but that civilization has brought with it vices and diseases, which threaten to exterminate the race unless checked.

Let us now turn our steps to South America, and we find in the section allotted to Chili, excellent books, maps, and drawings, tables beautifully inlaid with rich, native woods, and samples of fine marble.

In Peru there is a Panama hat which is almost as white and fine as if of linen, the price of which is $300. There is a most interesting piece of carving in sulphite of stone, cut three hundred years ago by native Peruvians. It represents the descent of Christ from the cross,—three men are taking down the body, while a woman is supporting the feet. Mary, the mother of Christ, stands by with clasped hands, looking at the bruised form, while another woman is prostrate on the ground with arms outstretched, as if in a paroxysm of grief and despair. The figures are somewhat crude, to be sure, but yet they express a wonderful conception of the subject, when we consider who the artists were. The figures are small, being only several inches in height.

We see also a Peruvian mummy, supposed to be three thousand years old, a hideous looking object, blackened and shriveled, the hair still preserved, and the tatooing on the wrist yet visible.   The remains are those of a female, and her shells, beads, iron ornaments, and long needles, as if for embroidery, were buried with her, ready for use in the land whither she had departed.   Some are found in earthen jars, some in wicker caskets, bound in coarse cloth like matting. Some have teeth like tusks, and must have been fearful looking creatures.   They are supposed to have been the founders of the Incas race.   The greater part of the space is taken up with the relics of the aboriginal races, although there are fine samples of wool, wines, and ores.

The Argentine Republic makes a very creditable display of leather, saddles, jars, beautiful tapestry, books, hair-work, wax flowers, laces, needle-work, and inlaid tables, which indicate a great scope of ingenuity and enterprise.

The little Orange Free State, the youngest nation in the world, I think, has an interesting department, in which are shown fine specimens, of leather, harness, ivory, ostrich feathers, and eggs, stuffed birds of the most brilliant colors, corals, and native woods of many beautiful varieties.

This completes our visit to the departments of the different countries in the main building.

But hear those shouts of laughter, peal following peal, the

CURIOUS PORCELAIN VASES. (p. 88.)

chorus led by the hoarse baying of some veteran in the warfare of life, mingled with shrill concatenations, boisterous outbursts from loud-voiced boys, mellowed by the silvery singing of girlish voices,—a perfect tornado of hilarity, as if all the mischievous imps of jollity had been let loose at once. Let us hasten with the hope that we may become likewise infected, and that our aching limbs and blistered feet may for a brief respite be forgotten, and the huge arches above us be rent in twain by the magnitude of our guffaws. We discover the cause of this irrepressible mirth, and we find that it consists in concave and convex mirrors, placed side by side on one of the main aisles, and in one moment you are contracted to a walking spindle, at the next you are broader than Dicken's Fat Boy, or the celebrated Daniel Lambert.

Here we see an exquisite statue of the Queen of Portugal, in marble, a calm, sweet, refined face, full of dignity and reserved power, her head-dress of rich lace work, admirably represented in the marble, the whole a beautiful piece of work. There is here an elevator which is driven by this little steam-engine near it, which is as large as a small room, and will carry thirty or forty persons at once. As we ascend, we gain a splendid view of the whole building as we look down over the gay spectacle, and we gradually withdraw from the ceaseless din, the steady roar of the immense multitude below. On the top of the building is a beautiful view of the surrounding country, the Schuylkill river, which gleams like a thread of silver through the waving forest; and between, the grassy hills,—villas, forests, and ridges glide away in the distance as far as the eye can reach. No more beautiful spot could have been selected for the great Exposition; and with our mind exhilarated by the inspiration of these natural beauties, we will descend and take our leave of this wonderful department.

And now we will pass to

The Annex to the Main Building.

We find this to be a large building filled with carriages, coaches, sleighs, domestic utensils, cars, engines, toys and machinery. A comparison of English carriages, with ours, shows theirs to be clumsier; in fact many of them are very heavy and cumbersome.

The following commission framed and hung up, shown by Messrs. Adams & Hooper, who are exhibitors, shows how the poor carriage makers hang on princes' favor. It smacks of red tape and sealing wax surely:

"I, Wm. Geo., Earl of Erroll, Master of the Horse to the Queen, do hereby appoint Messrs. Adams & Hooper to be

SCENE FROM TOP OF MAIN BUILDING.

coach makers to the establishment of her Majesty's stables during my pleasure.

"The quality and price of all articles supplied to this department will be strictly enquired into. The bill must be made up and delivered quarterly, to be examined and put in course of payment, and no Fee. Perquisite, or Poundage is to be given to the Clerk of her Majesty's Stables, or to any other person whatsoever.

Given under my hand, this 19th day of October, 1830, in the first year of her Majesty's reign.

[Seal.]

(Signed)   "ERROLL."

Russia exhibits some exceedingly fine work, amongst others a cutter, worth $230, made of ornamental wood and highly finished.

New England in the Olden Times.

Life in the olden time, in the days of the Puritáns, has been invested with such a halo of poetic interest by Longfellow, and other of our poets, that anything which gives us a true conception of it, is sure to be a great center of attraction. And so, when we see this log house, with wide, overhanging gables, small windows, and a rude but strong plank door,— the front yard gaily adorned by Sweet Williams, and the favorite posies of the long ago, and such a large crowd so anxious to gain admission, that it is necessary to have a bar across the gateway, and a policeman to keep back the throng, except at stated times, when he lifts up the bar, and allows such a limited number to pass through, as not to choke up the small rooms,— I say, when we see all this, we do not much wonder when we find that it is a reproduction of the old fashioned, genuine New England Home. We regard it with veneration, and enter it with reverence; for out of such homes have passed the men who have shaped and moulded the institutions of our country; have founded its colleges; made its laws: organized its states and municipalities, and made the wilderness to blossom as the rose. We pass through the low narrow door, and see the first thing, an old Almanac hanging on the wall. Now in those days, the almanac was an important part of family literature, and not only contained a calendar showing the time, but also wise proverbs, quaint sayings, and wholesome moral instruction. It may be a long time before we see so old an almanac again, so let us examine it more closely, and we shall see that it is a curiosity indeed. The title page begins "Almanac for year of our Lord Christ 1744, and from the creation of the world, according to the best of prophane history, 5694, and by the account of the Holy Scriptures 5646, by Nathaniel Ames;" followed by this poetic effusion:

"This little book serves well to help you date,
And settle many petty worldly things:
Think on the day writ in the book of fate
Which your own final Dissolution brings.
Millions have died the year thats past and gone,
And millions more must in the year to come."

On entering the room, we see the cradle in which Peregrine White was rocked, who was born on the Mayflower. It is made of oak, the sides and ends being rude panels, and has a canopy supported by small turned spindles, and looks durable enough to last for many generations to come. We can judge of the simple habits of life in those days, by this wooden platter 200 years old, which was in constant use during the Revolutionary war, and which is so plain and rude, that any rough craftsman could hew one out of a block.

Near it, we see an old flax wheel also 200 years old. One of the ladies in charge tells us, that several days ago, a very old man came in, and seeing this wheel exclaimed: "Why, this is just like the one my mother used to have!"—and his mind was carried back so vividly to the past, that he burst into tears, and could not control his emotion.

Here is a Revolutionary flag, which was borne in two regiments in the Revolutionary war. It is tattered and faded now, but must have been very beautiful when new. It is about three feet square, made of blue silk, with heavy gilt fringe, with a finely painted design of an eagle bearing a shield, also stars, and sunbeams, and a branch of holly, and the motto, "E pluribus unum." On a shelf is a silver teapot, plain and of moderate size, which was used by La Fayette in Boston; and there are also specimens of old blue porcelain covered with fantastic figures and designs, like those in which our grandmothers took so much pride.

It is strange what an interest gathers around these relics of the olden time. This is the writing desk of John Alden, that Puritan immortalized by the genius of Longfellow in the poem of "The Courtship of Miles Standish." It was brought in the Mayflower and is very small, being only about two feet high, a little more in length, and about ten inches in width. It is made of some dark colored ornamental wood, has pigeon holes, and two small drawers with large brass plates for handles, and large iron hinges.

Here is Gov. Endicott's chair, two hundred years old, very plain, and made of some sort of black wood.

On the wall is a deed signed by the sons of William Penn, in 1737. No printed blanks or short forms in those days, for the large sheet is closely covered by fine writing, in a precise, legal hand, and adorned with all the technical verbiage which characterizes old forms of legal documents.

There are few of us who are young, who have seen an old-fashioned fireplace, but who has not heard or read descriptions of them. Here is one with all its appendages,—the iron crane, with liberal facilities for numerous pots and kettles, (for we must remember they had large families in those days) its ample recesses large enough for huge logs to burn in, and the whole family to gather around; the andiron, frying pan, bellows, the shelf above, on which is arranged the pewter, the candlesticks, and many other articles of domestic use, while above it is swung the trusty rifle, powder horn and shot pouch, and yet above are strings of dried apples and pumpkins, which are hung in graceful curves.

But we find that the almanac did not exhaust all the literary aspirations of those days, for we see a large printed sheet, on which appears "A funeral elegy occasioned by the tragedy of ten persons drowned at sea." It has a lugubrious aspect, for at the top are a row of dismal black coffins, as if to prepare the reader for the sad recital which follows, and thus it proceeds giving us one of the

Specimen Poem of Colonial Times.

Awake my muse, and tune the song
  To harp a doleful sound,
Enough to melt the mournful throng
  Which echoes o'er the ground.

What heart but feels the heavy stroke
  Sent by God's awful hand,
When ten poor souls were lately cast
  Ashore upon the sands.

> Yes, ten poor souls I've heard them say,
>   Went lately to the bottom;
> Salem, O let it not be said
>   Their names were e'er forgotten.
>
> Hark, hark, we hear the passing bell
>   Along as they do go,
> Traveler stop, and shed a tear,
>   This is a scene of woe.

But we will turn from this painful narrative, and regale ourselves with a few specimen verses from some irrepressible bard of martial tastes, who thus inspires his comrades by his rollicking rhymes, which are entitled:

The Song of the Minute-man.

"Come rise up brother minute-men, and let us have a corous,
the bravei and the bolder, the more they will adore us;
oure country cals for Swords and Bals and Drums Aloud Doth rattle,
our fifers' charmes, arise to arms, Liberty cals to battle."

"We have some noble Congressmen, elected for our nurses;
and every joly farmer will assist us with their purses,
we let them stay at home we say, enjoy their wives with Pleasure;
and we will go and fight oure foes and save their lives and treasure."

"And when we Do return Again it will be with Glory,
for them that do remain at home to hear a valyant story;
they will draw nere and glad to hear not Doubting of the wonder
that minute men, though one to ten, should bring the tories under."

This too, was printed on a large sheet as if made to frame; and thus its patriotic spirit be transmitted to posterity. The New England Home would not be complete, unless the wo-

men of the olden time were represented; and here they are
with immense, starched, white net caps high behind, and
trimmed with gay ribbons, wide Vandyke capes or collars of
white material, and gaily figured dresses with very short
sleeves, and skirts of different colors; all making a jaunty and
picturesque costume. What garrets must have been ran-
sacked, what trunks and band-boxes, venerable with the dust
of decades, must have been ruthlessly despoiled, and their
forgotten contents resurrected, in order to revive in this Centennial year the wholesome memories of the olden time.

Uncle Sam's Government Building.

This building, though moderate in size, when compared
with the main building, is yet a large one, and filled with articles of great interest.

Let us notice some of the most remarkable of these. Here are
wonderful sets of apparatus used, in the signal service system,
by which the probable temperature of the weather is foretold. These models show the different plans of building light-
houses; some to float on the water, some built on a very
strong frame-work of iron, and others built of solid masonry
from the bottom of the water, by means of what is called a

coffer dam, which is a tight inclosure all around the space where the foundation is to be laid; and then the water is pumped out, so that men can work at the bottom.

Did you ever see a revolving light from a light-house, which can be seen ten or fifteen miles, and which the sailor recognizes from the colors of the light, and the number of revolutions per minute? Here is a very fine specimen, for the most dangerous places. It is about nine feet high, and six feet wide, large enough for a man to walk inside around the lamp, which is not very large, but has a circular wick about four inches in diameter. The sides are octagon, but they are not made of plain plates of glass, but of a great many bars of finely polished glass, which are placed at such angles, as to reflect the light in the best manner; and these are of different colors on each side. There are about fourteen of these large lamps used at present; and they can be seen for twenty-five or thirty miles.

One of the most famous feats in enginering in our day, was that of blowing up the submarine rock at Hell Gate, on East river, near New York. Before this was done, the depth at low water was only from two to five feet, and vessels, to avoid this, were in great danger of being caught by the current, and driven on rocks opposite to it, on the other shore. When this work is finished, and the broken rocks all taken out, the water will be about thirty feet deep, so that the larg-

UNCLE SAM'S GOVERNMENT BUILDING.

est vessels can pass over. There were about three acres of rock that were blown up, and here is a model that will show us how it was done. The top of the model shows us this coffer dam in a triangular form, the sides from one hundred to one hundred and fifty feet each, and also the bottom of the sea, in order to show the shallowness of the water, and what had to be done. The top of the model can be lifted up, and then we see that the rock below was honey-combed, and all taken out, except columns about twenty-two feet square, at regular intervals, which were were left to sustain the roof of rock, on which the water rested. All the vast amount of material which was blasted out, as well as water that soaked in, was taken and pumped out through the coffer dam.

But we will pass on, and notice these long rows of cases, containing models from the Patent Office at Washington. Over those, how many brains have ached, how many sleepless nights have been spent, how much poverty has been endured, how many fabulous fortunes have the sanguine inventors seen in them, almost in hand, and just ready to be grasped.

Here are case after case of specimens of ores and minerals, which would delight the heart of a geologist or mineralogist; also stuffed birds, animals, and fishes. See that immense white polar bear, nearly as large as an ox, and with such thick, heavy fur.

Here is a case containing Wasnington's camp chest, about sixteen inches wide by twenty-four in length, and ten inches high,—not a very large one for a commander-in-chief. It is covered by leather, and looks very old. There are compartments for lamps, medicines, and other things. You see also his set of table service while in camp. It is of the plainest pewter, with tin pots with wooden handles. Here is also his surveyor's compass, which he used in early life, and which looks very much like a common surveyor's compass, now used.

In this case are also many other articles which belonged to Washington, amongst which is a tea board, imported from France, made of ingrain wood-work of neat pattern; a heavy black thorn cane, with gold head, which was willed by Franklin to him; a very plain table about four feet long, and two and one-half feet wide, of dark wood; bed curtains which were embroidered by Martha Washington; two pistols, very large and heavy, with flint locks; his coats and breeches, which he wore when he resigned his command of the army,— the coat made of blue cloth, the sleeves and facings trimmed with white, the vest and breeches white, all having brass buttons, and being a very large suit, showing that he must have had a large and vigorous frame; and a fanciful picture, showing the pedigree of Washington, back hundreds of years, to one of the noble families of England.

Here is a queer specimen of a boat made by South Ameri-

can Indians.   It is like a large shallow washtub, about six feet
in diameter, and two feet deep; but is made of a rough frame
of wood, with sewed skins stretched over it.   There is only
one oar with it, having a paddle at each end.   We also notice
boats made by the Indians of British Columbia.   This dug-
out, which is about thirty feet long, is made of one log, and
very finely shaped; and those made of birch bark are well pro-
portioned, and skillfully constructed.   Here are wooden fish-
hooks made by the Sitka Indians, away up in Alaska.   They
are five or six inches long, and covered with carved images of
such horrid appearance, that the fishes must be hungry indeed, that could be tempted to bite them.   These large pieces
of bone, with pictures cut upon them, are teeth of the
Sperm Whale, which have been thus carved by sailors on
whale vessels; and very skillfully has it been done.   Here
is a full rigged ship, sails all set, and colors flying;
there is a figure of Bonaparte, and others of handsome female faces and figures.   They suggest tedious hours and
thoughts of loved ones at home; for poor Jack is proverbially
noted for a warm heart.

This immense boat about sixty feet long and eight feet wide,
is a dug-out, made from one tree, by the Indians of Vancouvers
Island.   The sides are left about six inches thick, and it is
painted inside, and bordered with red; and at the ends, are
painted rude heads, having large eyes.   It is a a fine, well

shaped boat, and looks as if it would do excellent service.

Here is a department showing the process of making muskets; and amongst other things, is this lathe for making the stocks. You see there is a pattern in the lathe, just like the stock to be made, and the chisel follows its surface, and turns the stock exactly the same shape. I presume you supposed the lock was let in the stock by hand, but here is a machine that does the work in a very short time. It is a very finely constructed piece of mechanism; having cutting tools like augers, which revolve swiftly; which are let down on the place to be cut, and guided by a pattern of the proper size and depth. We see the lock tried on the stock just taken out, and it is a perfect fit. It would have taken a good workman a long time to have done this by hand, and then it would not have been as well done. Let us notice these two old Spanish cannon, cast in the year 1400; and used by Cortez in the conquest of Mexico. They are made to load at the breech; for you see this bar can be taken out, a section of the cannon removed, the charge and powder placed in, and then the section put back again and held in place by the strong bar.

Here is a strange gun called the Gattling gun, after the inventor. It has ten barrels, somewhat larger than ordinary rifle barrels; and these are loaded at the breech by a sort of hopper, just large enough to hold a single column of cartridges. To discharge it, there is a crank which will turn three times in a minute, and fires three balls at each revolution. It is arranged so that it can be sighted; and some of larger size have an effective range of three or four miles. Another strange gun is called the " Coffee Mill Gun;" because it has a hopper about the same shape as that of a coffee mill, in which the cartridges are thrown. This has but a single barrel, and works with a crank; but is not a practical success like the other, as near as we can ascertain. All along this wall, you see hundreds of muskets, swords, cutlasses; and all sorts of arms used from very early times, down to the present day; and meant particularly to show the improvements made from time to time in implements of war-fare. Hours might be spent in looking over these old relics, and thinking over the bloody scenes in which they have taken a part. Here, for instance, is an old Roman sword, such as you see in pictures; short, straight blade, and brass hilt, and handle of a design to represent scales of fish.

You remember Paul Jones, the daring sea fighter, who won distinction as an officer in our navy, and who attacked and captured so many vessels belonging to Great Britain, during the war of 1812; and who is one of the most romantic characters in the annals of our naval warfare, and the favorite hero in numerous stories of desperate engagements and hair-breadth escapes;—well, here is his sword, this one, with rude blade which looks as if some common blacksmith had made it from an old cross-cut saw, and put it in that common oak handle, which any one could whittle out. But although rude, it was no less victorious, for the construction of the sword is of far less consequence than the hand that holds it, and the brain that directs it; and so, in the battle of life, victories are not so much gained by magnificent opportunities, as by making good use of those we have.

Here are wax figures of soldiers, showing the different uniforms of our army and navy, and the goods of which they are made. There are also, as you see, specimens of camp tents, also figures of horses, large as life, to show how artillery harness is constructed, and its quality. On one of them a cavalry man in wax is mounted, showing his uniform and equipments. Here, standing on end, are six beautiful bronze cannon, on which are brass plates, informing us that they were presented by Lafayette to the Americans during the Revolution. Two of them are about eight feet long, and the others about five feet long. They bear the stamp of Lafayette's coat of arms. Do you see that fine wax figure dressed in blue coat, with broad, white trimmings on cuffs and edges, and large brass buttons, white vest and gloves, leggings made of fine, strong cloth, and black, three-cornered hat, with colored plume on it? That was the uniform of Washington's Life Guards, and a very handsome one it was. But here is another of an old man with determined face,

THE MINUTE MAN.

dressed in homespun linen shirt, red vest, brown leggings and cloak, black stockings, and soft hat, and holding an old fowling piece in his hand. That is the minute man of 1776, half soldier, and half citizen.

But here we come to a spot where every student and American will tread tenderly. In this case is a marble statue, showing a fine intellectual head, with large brain, high forehead, long, curling hair, nose large, a firm mouth covered by a mustache, and a chin in keeping with the other characteristics of the face; and we see the name of Dr. Elisha Kent Kane, the famous Artic explorer. Who that has read the graphic and beautiful narrative of his life and experience in that land of eternal desolation, of the hardships and dangers, worthily undertaken and bravely endured for the cause of science, will not look on this cold marble with feelings of almost affectionate interest, especially those to whom that narrative was alike a revelation, and a romance.

In another case near by, we see the Esquimaux dress he wore, made in the fashion of the country, of the fur of the white polar bear, and covering the whole body, except the face; making a man look very much like a bear walking on his hind limbs. The rifle he used is also in this case,—an ordinary looking one, and above, we see his "kayah," or Esquimaux boat. They have also his sledge, made of pieces of wood fastened together with raw hide, and the runners shod with smooth pieces of bone, which are also fastened in the same way. The cross pieces on the top are also strongly tied on, and the whole is nothing but a simple frame.

Outside of the building, there stands a curiosity in the shape of an old army wagon, which was in the Union service four years and nine months, and has traveled 4160 miles. It has been through all the campaigns of Gen. Sherman, and though old, and battered, still looks as if it were good for several more campaigns.

One of the most interesting places, especially for those who have any love for antiquities, is a very large collection of Indian relics, from Mexico, Peru, California, and many of the Western and Southwestern States. Here are case after case filled with the most grotesque idols,—all with big, mis-shapen heads, and a severe burlesque on the human body; jars of many patterns, and of different colors, and some that are double, having a sort of Siamese-twin connection between them, and constructed so as to make a whistle. Then there are large pots and cooking utensils, of all sizes, generally black looking, and rude, but still well burned, and durable; stone hammers and pestles for crushing their grains; stone hatchets made of hard flint, to be fastened to wooden handles, spears and arrow heads, of many sizes and patterns, and some things that would puzzle any one to guess what they were made for, except for the purpose of bewildering and befogging the minds of speculative antiquarians, for which scarcely any improvement could be suggested.

These cases are arranged not with reference to the localities from which the relics came, so much as a classification in regard to the time when they were made, so that in one case, we may find articles from Mexico, California, or Michigan, or half a dozen places widely separated from each other. We notice a column of large idols, one carved above the other, on immense door posts from the houses of the Sitka Indians. They are very rude, and painted in glaring colors. Here is a genuine Indian wigwam, made of smoked buffalo skins, which is about sixteen feet in diameter, and has a hole at the top for the smoke to escape. There are also wax figures of celebrated Indian braves, with names indicating their blood-thirsty dispositions, and terrible fighting qualities. They are gayly caparisoned with all that can delight the Indian taste; paint without stint, war feathers, colored blankets, huge coils of beads, buckskin leggings, and fancy moccassins. Novelists with unsubdued fancies, may sit in their cozy back parlors, and write pretty little stories of the noble red man, bounding over his native wilds in all the untrammelled freedom of his irrepressible nature, his mind simple and confiding, his life full of romantic exploits,—and pen their fanciful life pictures, in which eagle plumes, brandishing tomahawks, dusky maidens, peaceful pursuits of the chase, charming simplicity of primitive life, and all the other accessaries of primal innocence and native chivalry, all find their appropri_ ate place; but let one of these red gentlemen, with his small, cruel, black eyes, his coarse, unkempt locks, and the charms of his wide cheek bones, and large animal mouth, heightened by a skillful application of red and yellow ochres; I say, should this attractive creature meet our charming story writer on those same native wilds, I fancy the next novel, if by some miraculous interposition of Providence it should be permitted at all, would indicate a very sudden change of base on the Indian question.

Here are thousands of specimens in mineralogy and natural history, brought from the Smithsonian Institute at Washington, which would be sufficient to occupy a student in those departments for months; but which we, without any special tastes in that direction, will pass over.

In a safe, are shown specimens of gold from Montana,— nuggets like peas, sticking from the quartz rock, in the most tantalizing manner, and many specimens of different sizes from gulch mines, and dust of many different degrees of fineness;— all making a fine exhibit of the untold wealth hidden in those wild mountains. A large torpedo is a noticeable object, about thirty feet long, pointed at both ends, with a propelling screw at one end, to drive it through the water. It is about three feet in diameter in the middle, is painted white;

THE ARIZONA METEORITE.

and is exploded by electricity. Hung up over the articles on exhibition, are many portraits, taken from public archives, of many of the most famous officers of the service, who have distinguished themselves by their valor, and whose memories are thus preserved, and held sacred by a generous and appreciative government.

Here is a machine for cutting cloth for army uniforms, which attracts much notice. The tailor takes perhaps twenty thicknesses of cloth, and chalks the pattern on the upper one, and this machine will cut through the whole thickness as clean as a pair of shears would cut a single piece, thus saving the labor of many men. We can get a very good idea of the immense size of the sperm whale, by noticing these jaw bones, forming an arch, each side about fourteen feet long, and nine feet of it being covered by teeth which are five or six inches long, and about two inches through. Here is also a model showing the perils of whale fishing, in which one of these hugh monsters has seized a boat in his jaws, and the sailors are floating about here and there, while the sea is lashed into a furious foam. On the the outside of the building are many kinds of cannon, one of which is a Rodman gun, about twenty feet long, and five feet in diameter at the butt, and it weighs 115,100 ℔s. It throws a shot weighing 1,080 ℔s., more than half a ton, and requires a charge of 200 ℔s of powder. It is mounted on a carriage, and is loaded at the muzzle. Another large gun is suspended from a frame by strong iron bars, and some hold, that this is the best mode of mounting such large pieces. It is very simple and inexpensive certainly, in comparison with the other method. A turret of a monitor is also to be seen, the sides protected by heavy plates of iron, and the mouths of the heavy cannon to be seen at the port holes. It is about fifteen feet high and perhaps thirty feet in diameter.

We can see the medical department in a separate building near by, where there are models of floating and permanent, hospitals, showing the inside arrangements with regard toconvenience, ventilation and furniture. Also models of ambulances, and all the appurtenances of hospital service. There are pictures on the wall which show all sorts of surgical operations, some of the most fearful character, which would seem impossible to perform, and the poor patient survive. There are some of the of most powerful microscopes here,—one of them shows a piece of a cat's intestine, a little larger than a pin's head, and the little capillaries are injected with Prussian blue and carmine; and it appears several inches in diameter, and is one of the most beautiful things you can imagine, having a ragged and irregular appearance, and colored with the most delicate tints. The officer in charge tells us that it requires the greatest skill to prepare such a subject for the microscope, and that very few are seen as perfect as this. In another microscope is a similar piece of a calf skin, and it looks like delicately tinted frost-work.

Not far from this, is a building filled with apparatus for preserving life at sea. There are all kinds of life boats, and life preservers, and a very interesting object is a mortar, by which they throw a coil of rope to a vessel in distress at a distance; and after a strong rope is fastened to the vessel and the shore, there is a sort of a cradle or basket which they pull by ropes to and from the ship, and thus save many valuable lives. The mortars used for this purpose are of different sizes, according to the distance they wish to send the rope. There is a short coil of wire fastened to the ball and the rope is tied to this, so that when the ball is fired, the sudden motion will not break the rope, but will merely straighten the wire, and in this ingenious manner the rope is prevented from breaking. There is another feature of the Government department which will make itself heard in spite of every thing, and that is an ear-splitting fog-horn, that every now and then bellows its discordant tones with startling effect.

The Women's Pavilion.

This department is by itself, in a tasteful building designed for the purpose, and is filled by needle work, embroidery, shell work, carving, paintings in oil and water colors, woven fabrics, drawings, and printing, all done by women of Spain, Japan, Great Britain, several Indian tribes, Sweden, the Phillipine islands and perhaps some other countries. Several looms are busily at work, attended by women, one of which weaves Centennial badges or book marks of very pretty design, which are readily sold as fast as made.

Queen Victoria has contributed some embroidery done by herself, also some of her etchings, as well as some drawings in pencil, of the Princess Louise, which are executed very pret-, tily, and show that they must have devoted considerable attention to these pursuits. So we see the greatest and best Queen of modern times, lending her influence and example to the cause of industry and labor.

In contrast with this, are some figures cut out of white paper without a pattern, by squaws of Iowa Indians, to be used for patterns in embroidery. They are cut in the most regular manner, having graceful figures, and displaying great skill and inventive thought. There are also dolls made by the squaws of the Winnebagoes, which are very neat and creditable. An elaborate pattern of lace, which has been partially made in the convent at St. Augustine, shows the process by which it is made. The pattern is marked out by pins, stuck so as to show the design, and hundreds of handles or spools, on which the thread is wound, have to be manipulated,

PHILADELPHIA U.S. AMERICA
MAY 10TH & NOVEMBER 10TH 1876.
1776
1876
WOMEN'S PAVILION,
INTERNATIONAL EXHIBITION

which must be a bewildering task. There are fine displays of the richest laces, the most brilliant wax flowers, and exquisite shell work. In one case are moccasins, smoking pouches, bow case, quiver, belts, etc., all made by Indian women, and displaying great ingenuity.

A carpet loom is in operation, weaving an elaborate pattern of ingrain carpet, and worked by a woman. A lady artist of Cincinnati, Mrs. Mary G. Este, has executed an exquisite bas-relief in butter of "Iolanthe," the blind daughter of a king, which is one of the most beautiful works of art in the department. There are wonderful specimens of painting in colors on china, by amateurs, which are truly admirable. Also several pieces of wood carving, which must convince anyone that a large part of this work may be transferred to women, and thus her sphere of labor enlarged. We also notice several pieces of painting on silk, which are extremely beautiful.

Several groups of wax figures from Sweden, are very interesting, and give an excellent insight into the peculiar characteristics of the people in regard to features and costume. One, is that of a maiden, who is picking a flower, to ascertain what answer she shall give her lover, who stands behind her leaning forward with an expression of great earnestness, and looking over her shoulder to learn the result. Another maiden at her side is looking on with great interest also to see the fate of her friend. They have the wide cheek bones, rather flat nose, and straight, flaxen hair, which are generally characteristic of the people.

The Japanese ladies have contributed a piece of exquisite needlework, being the portraits of the royal family of Japan. There are cases of gold embroidery which are extremely rich, and some of the oil paintings are works of great merit.

Education Among the Japanese.

Japan has an educational department, which does her infinite credit, and shows the enterprise and activity of that wonderful people in this direction. It is an extensive collection of school books, maps, charts, school registers, pictures chemical and philosophical apparatus, examination reports, etc.

From a very intelligent Japanese gentleman, who speaks quite good English, who is dressed in our costume, tall silk hat and all, and who has charge of this department, we learn that Japan has a system of public schools, in which they have substantially adopted the American method of education. Their system is compulsory, requiring the attendance of children from six to fifteen years of age, and at the present time, sixty per cent. of the children of proper age are in actual attendance. They have fifty thousand of these public schools, which are supported by the Government and are free to all. They have also an Imperial University, under the care of the Government, in which are taught the English, French, German, Russian and Chinese languages, chemistry, the higher mathematics, and literature. A law school is also connected with this, and is a part of the University. They have also established kinder-garten schools within the past year, on much the same plan as carried on in this country. He tells us that the Japanse alphabet contains forty-eight letters, and there is no sound which a letter will not represent; that there is a regular arrangement of sounds corresponding to our vowels and consonants; that some words are composed of a single letter, that the Chinese and Japanese languages are entirely distinct, although of late years many Chinese words have crept into common use, and have become incorporated in their Japanese languages, the same as foreign words with us. They have a counting machine, with which they can add together numbers with great facilty. It is like an abacus, having five wires about two feet long stretched horizontally in a frame, with a large number of button-like pieces of wood strung on them. With this they will add together large sums sooner than we can, with pencil and paper. As an experiment, I gave the numbers 3,654 and 7,322, and the result was given, before I could set them down and add them together.

A large case of chemical and philosohical apparatus is exhibited, entirely of Japanese manufacture, but most of it is a mere imitation of ours; as they had very little of their own, before their country was opened to foreigners. This apparatus is seemingly as accurate and well made, as that used by our institutions of learning. We see here primers with pictures opposite the letters, to illustrate them, as in ours. Specimens of map drawing are shown, which would be considered excellent in our schools; one in particular of the United States, the States being nicely colored, and the lettering neatly done in English.

There are a number of colored pictures which are interesting, as they show the difference between the old and the new methods of teaching. The old method was for the pupils to sit in groups on the bare floor, with their feet curved under them like tailors, and their books lying on the floor before them, while the teacher, who is an important looking personage in venerable robe, also sits in the same manner with a pile of books by his side; and this was also the old way in giving lectures. The pictures showing the present school-rooms, show convenient desks, comfortable seats, black-boards and maps on the wall, a neat desk for the teacher on an elevated platform, and all the conveniences of a well appointed school-house. There are excellent charts shown, for students of natural history, representing all kinds of birds, animals, plants, fishes, and fruits; and, also, cases of stuffed birds, beasts, fishes and insects. Also pictures of articles of domestic use, to be used as object-lessons. To give some idea of the intelligence and cast of mind of the Japanese scholar, and also, to preserve as a literary curiosity, we will copy a composition written by a Japanese school-boy about fifteen years old, in the first class of the junior division; which is entitled,

Auto-biography of a Sword.

"I was born in a solitary place, under an elevation of land, "where I hardly could breathe the pure air and enjoy the de- "licious sunshine—like persons confined in a dark prison. "My house was just as long as my person; from this account, ' I grew never larger; although, I remained there for a long "time I longed for a helper in getting out of this unpleasant "place, confiding my fate in the Great Father Above. But "the Providence was cold towards me for a long time; but "after the lapse of years and years, a kind, strong man came "in search of me. He dug the ground over and took me up to "the open air. He appeared to be very kind, yet I knew not "what he intended to do with me.

" I, indeed, was half in fear, and half in joy,when the kind
" but fearful looking man said with his thundering voice:
" 'You must be submissive to me, and become what I wish you
" to.' I trembled with fear and joy, and could not utter any
" other word, but yes.

" I accompanied him to his house, which was very large and
"pleasant for me, and within a few days, I witnessed him to
" be my real benefactor. My joy was as great as mountains, for
"I was treated very kindly. He appeared to be eager in edu-
" cating me well; and, indeed, he was, for at the age of twenty
"I received the rank of Sword, from the brilliancy of my
" mind, strong will, valor, strength and the respectful coun-
" tenance which I wore. These qualities soon made me up
" to become the subject of a great Sammai (probably the offi-
" cial rank of the master). I defended him always from his
" enemies, and frequently went to battle with him.

" But I felt sometimes very dangerous, particularly when
" he brandished my body around his fearful enemies,—over
" precipitous rocks, one time throwing me upon hard iron
" armour, and the other upon the heads of his enemies. Thus
"I served my master for a long time, and now I remain
" useless, reclining to the setting of my long life, becoming
" old and infirm; and the descendants of my master too, re-
" main now unoccupied, and in a poor condition."

We will copy also the composition of a little Japanese

school-girl in second year, junior course. It is written apparently in her handwriting in English, in a plain hand, and may be entitled

A Story of the Wolf and Mouse.

"There was a wolf which was sleeping. A little mouse
"came then and crept on the nose of the wolf. Then the
"wolf was very angry. and said, 'I am very angry and I will
"kill you.' The little fellow tremblingly said, 'Sir, I was
"wrong; pardon me if you please.' But the fierce fellow
"could not hear what the little fellow said. The poor fellow
"said again, and again, five times. At last the wild fellow
"forgave him, telling him to begone. The little fellow went
"away feeling very happy. One day when the wolf was
"going in search of food, he was caught by a trap, and he
"was very wretched and unhappy. Then the little fellow
"came there, and said, 'Thou hast spared my life three or four
"days ago; therefore, I will now return favor to you.'

"And the little mouse gnawed the strong string with her
"small and sharp teeth. Then the wolf was very glad, and
"he thanked the mouse. If even brutes learn to return favor
"to men or their mates, by whom once aided, therefore when

"our friends are wretched, we must help them; and we
"must return favor to our parents."

(signed) Y. OISHI.

Can it be possible that the little Japanese girl had
read, or heard, the fable of the lion and the mouse in old
Æsop's fables, which it resembles so much? If not, it is a
production of striking originality, and would do honor to an
older head.

For the purpose of showing more fully the inner life and
thought of these strange people, as well as their mental cali-
bre and intellectual activity, we will examine still another
specimen. It is an essay from an ambitious young man in
the law department of the Imperial University, who aired
his powers of logic and argumentation by the following dis-
sertation on this subject:

The Contrast between Self-Love (or self-Interest) and Selfishness.

"It requires great care in any one, lest self-interest, and
"selfishness, should be confounded together. For in respect
"to the effects which result from the exercise of each, regard-
"ing motives, the two courses of actions induced by such

"impulses would differ greatly, and would sometimes be op-
"posed to each other. However, the line of demarkation
"drawn between them is somewhat obscure, and so it is very
"difficult to determine where such line is to be found, and
"thus a man of uncultured mind is very apt to fall into
"error.

" Self-interest seeks to promote one's own interest and hap-
"piness in the main, that is to say, it aims at the safety and
"liberty of his person, the security of his personal property,
"and the improvement of his character. Indeed it is his
"right to secure his liberty and person, which are inherent
"in him at his birth, and the enjoyment of his private property
"which he may have lawfully acquired. For this purpose
"he might reasonably make any effort whatever, so that it
"does not injuriously affect the rights of others.

" Although self-interest aims directly at ones own interest
"or happiness, yet it does by no means neglect the interest
"of others. Thus the object of self-interest is to promote
"one's own happiness without causing any injury to the in-
"terest of another.

" On the other hand, selfishness has a strong bias to regard
"exclusively one's own interest, or rather satisfaction; or to
"use more strong language, it neglects altogether, the in.
"terest of others for the sake of his own interest alone. The
"natural consequence is, that the others suffer an injury

"thereby. At all events its motives are base and mean, and "so are to be condemned altogether. Thus it is clear that "selfishness is merely self-interest going too far beyond its "proper limit.

" We shall now conclude the subject by bringing the two "in contrast, thus: self-interest regards his own interest as "well as that of the others, whereas selfishness neglects that "of others entirely. The end of the one is admirable, whereas "that of the other is low and mean; the motive of the one "is reasonable, whereas that of the other is sinful; the one "producing good effects upon all, whereas the other brings "injury upon the rest of mankind."

We see by this, that the Japanese are by no means blind, as regards the knowledge and perception of moral obligations.

Next, suppose we visit

PHILADELPHIA U. S. AMERICA
MAY 10TH – NOVEMBER 10TH 1876.
1776
1876
MACHINERY HALL.
INTERNATIONAL EXHIBITION

The Wonders of Machinery Hall.

Perhaps you have a taste for mechanics and inventions,—suppose then we take a walk through Machinery Hall. Here we see an immense building that would make old Vulcan dance with joy, so many are the machines of various kinds which it contains, and so diversified their uses. Here is a tobacco establishment where they are making cigars regularly, and the four negro workmen make the air vocal with their old plantation melodies or camp-meeting choruses. Hear how their clear musical voices ring out far above the clatter of looms and the whir of machinery, and cause a crowd to gather around, delighted to hear the unexpected musical treat. See this paper mill of such immense size and complicated machinery. Did you ever wonder how the clean white paper, so pure and fresh, is made from pulp of old rags, and vegetable fibre? Here is the long row of rollers through which it passes, starting at one end as pulp, and coming out at the other as firm, strong, white paper.

Speaking of paper, did you never wonder how wall paper was made; so elegant in design, of so many colors, and yet so cheap. This large cylinder about ten feet high, and framework about sixty feet long, is the machine for making it, and we see them printing a roll of paper of elaborate pattern, in fifteen different colors; and all those colors are printed while passing through the machine once. Notice that for each color, there is a roller with the pattern cut upon it like type, and this is wet by a roll of flannel which passes through a trough containing the proper color, and so each roller does its work in turn, and the paper appears on the frame complete, and dries as it reaches the end of the long line of rollers.

Let us stop and examine this method of painting on china and porcelain. This man with the head of an artist, and a firm, skillful hand, will paint your name so perfectly, that you would imagine it to be stamped on by machinery; or he will paint one of those beautiful heads that you see on those china cups standing near by.

We have often wondered how railway car wheels can go so far, without breaking or wearing out. Think of the millions of times they revolve in going from New York to San Francisco, over switches, cross roads, defective rails, up and down grades, around curves, rushing on with a speed that almost makes us shut our eyes and hold our breath, and yet how few accidents occur from the breakage of wheels; so let us stop and look at this pair of car wheels, which have run 460,000 miles, and have worn out three axles and are on the fourth, and which are good for 75,000 miles more service.   It is decidedly comforting to think of their wearing qualities.

Here is a flouring mill all complete and no larger than a sugar hogshead.   The wheat goes in at this hopper, is ground by burr stones, and in this trough comes out the fine white flour, at one end the shorts, and in another trough the bran.   By raising the cover, we can see the bolts.   This mill can be worked by steam or horse power, and six horse power will run through seven bushels of wheat per hour, or it can be changed so as to grind corn or buckwheat.   Think of a complete flouring mill for $400, and then feel thankful once more that you live in this Centennial year. `

You may rest assured that wherever you see a crowd assembled, there is something interesting going on, and here we find the attraction to be the manufacture of rubber shoes. Perhaps you have thought the rubber is taken from the tree and put into a machine which turns out the shoes already made and marked for sale; if so, you are slightly mistaken, as you may observe.   In the first place, there is a machine for spreading a coat of rubber over netting, which is elastic.   This is cut ready for the last, by that man over there; and this girl then fits it to the last and puts on a rubber covering. Another takes it, trims it off, coats the bottom with a kind of paste, and then puts on a rubber sole, which she trims so dexterously and quickly, that it is a pleasure to see her.   Then they are put in that oven over there, where they are vulcanized,—then they are polished and receive the finishing touches.

Here is a working model of a railroad car run by compressed air. It ascends a steep grade, and passes from one end of the track to the other, but needing to be supplied quite frequently with compressed air from a fixed reservoir.

Yachting is becoming a popular recreation for millionaires of nautical tastes,—shall we examine this model of a steam yacht? You see it is only about four feet long and nine inches wide, and yet, a little steam engine working inside, is driving the little brass screw wheel at the stern. A beautiful piece of mechanism truly, and constructed apparently on the most approved methods of marine architecture, when a high rate of speed is desired.

Here also is a working model of a U. S. monitor, with revolving turret and guns, and steam engine driving the propelling screw.

But what a clatter is here, and a crowd pressing forward to get a sight of the wonder. And it is a wonder, over which orators might rhapsodize, and poets grow wild, and which, if a man had dreamed of one hundred years ago, he would have been considered a lunatic. It is one of Hoe's presses, printing a newspaper at the rate of 480 copies per minute. That means, one at every eighth of a second, printed on both sides, folded twice, and laid in piles, ready for the counter or newsboy. And you see the machine does it alone,—all it needs is to be started, and the papers taken away. The press is fed from the roll, as you see, which is like a very large spool on which the paper is wound. And yet this marvellous machine which produces such wonderful results, requires so little power, that one of the workmen tells us, that it could be turned by one man.

But there we notice another crowd, and consequently there must be something interesting going on. This proves to be quite a large machine, which is worked by a little girl, who is winding silk from the cocoon. The cocoons are put in a sort of vat of hot water, to loosen the silk, then the threads are attached to reels which are turned by power, and the little girl keeps the threads in order. You may think this a very simple operation, but if you tried to do it, you would find it a very hard matter, and a process which requires a great deal of judgment and experience. Look at this case and see the rich, creamy colored silk in rolls, as it has been taken from the reels, and ready to be wrought into the most costly and beautiful fabrics.

We come now to a spot decidedly warlike in aspect, and look up and find that we are within the confines of Russia. The great bear means to convince us that he is not behind other powers of the earth in his military accoutrements, and so, here we see an enormous cannon about sixteen feet long and about three feet in diameter at the largest end, with a bore of about twelve inches, which will carry a ball weighing 300 lbs. seven and one-half miles (at least, so the black-whiskered Russian in charge informs us); also this large brass cannon about nine feet long and two and a half feet thick at the base, having a bore of about nine inches, and which will carry a large ball probably three or four miles. Here are many other specimens of smaller brass and iron field pieces, all finely mounted, and kept in the most perfect order. These figures of four horses of natural size, are models showing mounted artillery. Here is a small cannon, taken apart, and carried with all its appurtenances on pack saddles on these horses. They show also, specimens of their army wagons, and of their boats and life boat. The life boat seems to be constructed on the same principle as one adopted by our government, which is made of two cylinders of very strong air tight cloth, about twenty feet long and two and a half feet in diameter, filled with air, with a framework between them, of wood, upon which the navigator stands, but it is only to be used as a life boat, as there would be no dry place on it. The other boats exhibit the highest skill in boat building, both as to shape and finish. Here is one made of two long narrow boats like canoes, placed apart four or five feet, and fastened together with a seat between them.

But we now come to Sweden, and can have opportunity to

judge of her skill in mechanical appliances. These immense machines are saw mills, some with upright, and some with circular saws, and seem so strongly built, as if to last ages. Here are models of ancient armor, covered with rich designs, which have been pressed into shape by powerful dies, and here are specimens of her heavy castings, which show that she is not behind her rivals in this department.

France has a great variety of machinery on exhibition, some of which we will notice. She is justly noted for her silk weaving, and here we can see the operation. The loom is very simple, and made mainly of wood, but the fabrics it produces are of the heaviest and richest kind. This loom is probably the same in design as those used by the Huguenots centuries ago, and on which were made those woven goods that were famous throughout Europe.

But here we come to a monster machine, which is used for sinking shafts, for mines or wells. The frame is about forty feet high, and this ponderous affair, which looks like a weight, is a drill weighing several tons, which has chisels at the bottom, and which is raised by hoisting apparatus to the top of the frame, and then is dropped down in the shaft, where the chisels loosen and cut the rock. This immense pair of pincers, like fingers interlacing each other, is to lower down and catch the loose material which the drill has made. Another machine is so ·massive that it would make a good sign for old Vulcan's forge,—it is a sugar mill for grinding the cane; having enormous rollers about ten feet long, and three feet in diameter, between which the cane passes, crushing out, we should suppose, every particle of moisture. They are attached to a cog-wheel, which is driven by another immense cog-wheel about twenty feet in diameter, and this is regulated by a very heavy balance wheel of about the same diameter. This is some of the most powerful machinery shown, and is almost sublime in its massiveness.

But now we come to Brazil, that growing empire, which makes such a magnificent display in many departments of the Exposition, and whose ruler seems to feel so great an interest in our country. Here we see in models, the uniforms of the Brazilian army, some of linen, and some of blue cloth, with less gilt lace and embroidery than some, but yet quite as substantial and serviceable. Here are many pieces of cannon, and models which give us a very clear idea of their army equipments, baggage wagons, pontoon bridges, ammunition wagons, and ambulances. A steam engine, highly finished, and working in the most perfect manner, attracts our attention; also beautiful models of sections of machinery, amongst which, is one of a monitor, which shows that the enterprising Emperor does not mean to be left behind in the appliances for marine warfare.

But here again is a large crowd, anxiously pressing forward

to catch a glimpse of some strange thing. It proves to be an envelope machine, and it is truly a marvel of ingenuity. Can you imagine a machine that will pick up a piece of paper, the upper one of a large pile, already cut in proper shape, fold it on four sides, print a stamp or card on it, and pass it along, until twenty-five are collected and dropped in a box, ready to be wrapped into a package by the girl who works the machine, and yet, all this is done with the accuracy and precision of clockwork.

Another envelope machine performs still greater marvels, and may be justly ranked as one of the most ingenious pieces of mechanism ever invented. A coil of white paper, as wide as the length of the envelope is placed at one end of the machine, taken into it and comes out again perfect envelopes pasted with mucilage, and ready for use. They are made at the rate of one hundred and twenty per minute, and delivered in packages of twenty-five each, ready to be bound for sale. I will not attempt to describe the ingenious mechanism, but the envelopes pass over eleven large wheels in order to give them time to dry, and all the parts work with such precision, that they almost seem endowed with brains.

Let us stop a moment and examine this strange looking frame, with two sails on it, full rigged. We find it to be an ice yacht, about thirty feet long, and perhaps twenty feet wide at the extreme. It is all frame, there being only room enough at the stern for about two persons to sit upon. It is mounted on runners, and is rigged very much like an ordinary sail boat. We learn by the card fastened upon it, a strange fact if it be true, viz: that it will move faster than the wind, and the reason given is that it does not sail merely before the wind, but at some angle to it, and at every gust of wind receives an additional movement forward, and thus outstrips the wind itself. Whether this be so or not, it is claimed that it can make sixty miles an hour, and this would be fast enough to make ones brain reel.

But here is another crowd which almost blocks up the aisle, —let us see what is so interesting. It is a machine for sticking pins, worked by a young lady. It is difficult to imagine how pins thrown together loosely, the same as if shoveled from a bin, can be stuck on paper at the rate of 180,000 per day, and done with such order, and by one person. You see how this is accomplished; a small stream of pins runs down this kind of sluice-way, till they come to a narrow groove, just large enough for the body of the pin, but not large enough to let the head through; so most of them are soon hanging on this groove, which is a very apt illustration of what a witty Frenchman suggested, when he said that wise men were like pins, because their heads would not let them go too far. The pins then slide down to a place, where they are gradually laid in a horizontal position, where they are punched into the pa-

per, which is folded by the machine in the right form. Those
that do not fall into the groove, and fall over the sides of the
sluice-way, have to go through the same operation again, until they are properly stuck on the paper.

But this pin machine is little in point of inventive skill,
in comparison with this loom for weaving Brussels carpet.
How a man could ever invent such a machine, and keep from
a lunatic asylum is a mystery. Here are large cases, each full of
bobbins of differently colored threads, altogether about one
hundred, which are necessary to form the elaborate pattern of
the carpet. The loom starts with a great clatter, and you see
how the carpet comes, the pattern developing every moment.
Here are looms for weaving ginghams and plaids, and one is
here which will weave a piece of canvas about thirty feet wide,
as you see by a piece in it. This, however, is a coarse fabric,
and is used to make oilcloth. But here is the most wonderful
thing of all, in the way of weaving, and worth going miles
to see. It is this English loom that is weaving twenty pieces
of these wonderful book marks and badges, that are made of
the most brilliant colored silks, and designed with the greatest
taste. For instance, notice these in the loom: at the top of
each is a beautiful design of various colors with appropriate
lettering; then a very accurate portrait of Washington; then
the motto, "First in war, first in peace, and first in the hearts
of his countrymen;" then a view of one of the Centennial

Buildings, ending with a beautiful design of a shield decorated by flags,—all this woven thread by thread, in different colored silks, and twenty of them at a time, and you can perceive it is truly a marvel. It takes three hours to make them, so elaborate is the design.

On the stand you see other mottoes, of many other patterns. One with a piece of music, another with a bust of Shakespeare, another with a muster-roll of a division of the army—in fact there seems to be nothing too complicated for them to copy.

But let us turn a moment, from the ornamental to the useful. Do you see this ponderous lathe, in which shavings of iron can be turned as easily as you can whittle a pine shingle? Look at this immense iron planer, with platform about thirty feet long, and ten feet wide, on which the iron to be planed is bolted. See how it rolls from one end of the track to the other, running under a strong bar, fastened above, on which the cutting tools are fixed, and the bar is then let down to the iron on the platform, and the platform set in motion. This will plow a groove in a piece of iron, or plane a wide shaving, so easily, that you would not notice a tremor of the machine.

We see an immense hammer, weighing two and a half tons, with a striking power of fifty or sixty tons.

Here is a curiosity. Do you see that india rubber ball remaining almost stationary in the air, kept in place by a jet of compressed air? The jet of air is not thrown out upward, so that the ball is not directly above it, but at an angle of nearly forty-five degrees, and yet the ball is not driven off sideways, but keeps its place all the same. A wooden ball is exchanged for the rubber one, and yet it remains just the same, and we are told that an iron one would remain poised in the air in the same manner.

Here is a curious and useful contrivance. Do you see that drill, which turns so swiftly at the end of what seems to be a rubber rope, or tube? The secret is this. There is a flexible coil of wire inside the rubber tube, and this coil is attached to a shaft, and so turns the whole length, and drives the drill. So with this machine, they can drill a hole anywhere in a room, or apply it for any purpose where they wish to employ power in different places, such as polishing different pieces of marble, and many other purposes.

A steam engine is so common a thing, that we see them without any surprise, but here is one, that is worth a moment's attention. Notice this beautiful, silver plated engine, hardly larger than two barrels, set on end, and yet it has the power of two horses, and works as perfectly as possible. You see it scarcely requires more fuel than a common cooking-stove, but is powerful enough to drive many kinds of machinery, such as small printing presses, turning lathes, etc.

When you go over Suspension Bridge, at Niagara Falls, for

the first time, if you feel as I did, you will suddenly wonder what kind of iron ropes the bridge is made of. In order that you may know beforehand, let us stop here and see a short section of those wire ropes. Here it is, made of 3,640 wires, of pretty good size, and these make a large rope, about one foot thick, with a sustaining weight of 6,000,000 lbs. Probably you may have heard how a suspension bridge is now being constructed between New York and Brooklyn, over East river, so high, that vessels with tall masts, can pass under; and here we can see a section of the wire rope to be used there. It is made of seven thousand wires, about the size of ordinary fence wire, which make an immense rope, about one foot and a half thick, and strong enough to sustain the enormous weight of 22,300,000 pounds.

This powerful machine here, with such ponderous iron castings, seems to be for pressing cotton into bales. We knew that cotton was baled, but not that such immense power was needed to make the bales. Here is one, and you notice that the cotton is almost solid.

Here we come to a part of the hall, which, with the aid of a little imagination, we might think, was an enchanted palace. There are sewing machines of all patterns; silver plated, gilt, polished, lacquered, glittering like flashing jewels, as they swiftly whirl, while all around are beautiful wax figures, turned by automatic machinery, and showing on each side, the richest robes of white satin, or colored silks, covered by the most lavish embroidery of gilt lace, and reflecting all the hues of the rainbow.

Here are fire engines, painted in the most ornamental manner, and fairly ablaze with gilt and silver plating, and lustrous varnish.

This circular saw is said to be the largest in the world, and surely large enough for all purposes, except, possibly, to saw the big trees of California. It has a diameter of one hundred inches, and the teeth are like cruel fangs, fairly aching to let daylight into the heart of a solid log.

But now we have come to a piece of mechanism, which has become famous throughout the civilized world, and which has had a sublime part in the celebration of our centennial year. I refer to that monster with those great beams going up and down, first one, and then the other, ten feet up, and then ten feet down, hung up as high as a large barn, about thirty feet, the immense balance wheel, thirty feet in diameter, with a rim of solid iron, about sixteen inches square, and which makes a breeze, as it whirls around. See the ladders that go away up, on each side, to the top of the working beams, and up the sort of passage, that is railed off all around it, so that they can oil and repair it. As we see it move, we might imagine it to be old Thor, himself, with thews of steel, and heart of fire.   I heard one of the guards say, that when **Pres-**ident Grant, and Emperor Dom Pedro, of Brazil, opened the Exposition, they, at a signal, moved this lever, and the ponderous cranks and wheel started, as if instinct with life, and at that moment, five miles of machinery started at once into active operation; all along that five miles, the operators were standing ready for the signal, and in an instant, all were at work, the looms weaving their varied fabrics, the printing presses throwing off their sheets like huge snow flakes, and pumps, lathes, drills, hammers, and the wilderness of machinery, which you see around you, were humming, pounding, whirring, and clattering, a grand chorus and tribute to their unsceptered monarch,—" Industry."

But let us go toward that rushing sound of many waters, as if a hundred cataracts were falling, and we behold the pump department. Here is a reservoir, the size of a respectable pond, in which are poured about fifty streams of water, from pipes, from an inch, to a foot in diameter; and at the end, is a genuine waterfall, about thirty feet high, and the same in width, which sweeps over the verge, like a wide ribbon of satin, and in falling, breaks up into tassels. All the water for this waterfall, is raised by that little steam engine, below it, which, although small enough to stand in a room twelve feet square, has one hundred and twenty-five horse power, and is a model of simplicity, compactness, and power.

But let us see these huge machines on this side, which roar so loudly. We find that they are blowers, for pumping air in mines, and for creating a draft of air for blast furnaces, and are made by revolving fans in tight compartments, which make about three hundred revolutions a minute, which is so fast that you cannot see the arms whirl. Here is one which sends out such a strong current of air, that you cannot stand before it. Hold on your hat, and let us go up as near as we can. The air almost pounds our faces, and those wearing wigs, had better not try the experiment, for the air comes rushing out, like a concentrated hurricane.

Here is a a painting machine that will paint, it is claimed, eight hundred slats for blinds in an hour, and it is a small machine too, only about four feet high, and two feet square. The articles are passed through it, and come in contact with a revolving brush, which is supplied by paint in a trough.

Let us examine a moment this immense steam-wagon for road or farm work, which looks something like a railway locomotive. The wheels are about a foot wide, and rough, so that they will not slide on the ground; but it looks so heavy and cumbersome, that you would not think it could do more than move itself, but we are told that it has drawn twenty tons, and is made for plowing, driving thrashing machines, pulling stumps and many other purposes. It has sixteen horse power. Speaking of steam-wagons, you remember the steam-carriage we saw on the drive in Fairmount Park, driven by a small steam-engine behind, about as large as a barrel, guided by a man sitting in front, who turns the wheels as he pleases, and the carriage has room enough besides for about eight passengers,—one of the lighest, airiest affairs of the kind, that can be imagined. It seems to be perfectly manageable, as much so as a well broken horse, and can be turned as easily. The steam is turned down towards the ground, and makes but little noise, and I do not see why they can not be used for pleasure wagons, on park drives, or smooth roads.

But here we come to the German department, and every thing we see, gives us the impression of a vigorous and industrious people. Look, for instance, at this immense plate of iron, an inch and half thick, thirty feet long, and about four feet wide, or at this tremendous iron beam for bridge or building, about fifty feet long, and eighteen inches high; while all around are immense bars and bolts, and plates of iron of almost every size and weight, with specimens of their numerous ores. Here, also, is the famous Krupp cannon; and a giant it is truly, and looks as if it could sink the largest war vessel afloat. It is about thirty feet long, without the frame which extends back about fifteen feet farther, and is made to be securely fastened to the floor by strong bolts. At the base, it is about five feet thick, but is much smaller in diameter at the muzzle. It is a breach loader, and is made for a ship of war. In the rear, there is a platform and railing for the man to stand on who sights it, and it can be raised or lowered at pleasure, by turning these cranks, which are attached to very complicated looking machinery. The ball lies there by its side, about three and a half feet long, made of the hardest iron, pointed and about fourteen inches through. It weighs 550 ℔s, and is raised and moved to its place by this derrick at the side, which is turned by a crank. It throws this ball from fifteen to sixteen miles, and the weight of the cannon without the carriage, is fifty-nine tons.

See this enormous crank and shaft, for a steam-engine, which is about sixteen inches in diameter, and made of forged iron. Here, also, are models of mounted artillery, three horses being packed with a cannon taken to pieces, the size of the cannon being about four feet long, and six inches in diameter.

We come now to a strange looking engine. Perhaps you think that all engines are driven by steam; if so, you will see this is driven by another motive power. It is quite a large engine, having a balance wheel about six feet in diameter, and a rim four or five inches square, making a heavy amount of metal, and yet it is operated by that single gas jet, that you see burning at the bottom. Gas and air are burned in such proportions that a mild explosion takes place about every minute, sending a piston upward about a foot, which communicates the motion to the balance wheel, and gives it a power equal to two horses.

Now we have reached the department of Great Britain; and we see again all around us, the most powerful machinery for working iron. Look at this machine for cutting iron; that strong thick blade which rises and falls so majestically, will cut a bar of cold iron an inch and a quarter thick, and four inches wide, as easily as you can work a pair of scissors. This enormous hammer which weighs two and a half tons, and has a striking weight of from fifty to sixty tons, is made for forging heavy iron, and can be made to work as softly as a lady tapping your shoulder with her fan, or to thump hard enough as to almost deafen your ears, and shake the whole building.

Here is a curiosity; it is this section of steel armor plate, nine inches thick, the same as used in plating the outside of war vessels; but this has been fired at, from a distance of thirty feet, by a pointed rifle ball, seven inches in diameter, and made of the hardest chilled iron, harder than steel, and charged by fourteen pounds of powder. See those great holes about eight inches deep, in the hard steel, which the balls made. Here is another plate, eight inches in thickness, which has been fired at from the same distance, with a round ball weighing sixty-eight pounds, and charged with thirteen pounds of powder, and the dents are only about an inch deep. That last pound of powder, and the ball being round

BIG HAMMER.

instead of pointed, makes a wonderful difference in the effectiveness of the shot.   Here is a man in charge of the machinery who has the face of an inventor, and I venture to say, is a natural mechanic,—let us ask him a few questions.   He tells us that this machinery for the manufacture of iron, is destined to work a revolution in the iron interests of this country, so perfectly does it do its work.   He also tells us that this piece of armor plate, made of steel fourteen inches thick, is used for plating war vessels, and that Great Britain has two vessels plated with armor steel twenty-four inches in thickness, and wonderful to say, that they have recently fired a ball entirely through it, from an enormous cannon, weighing eighty tons without the carriage, the most powerful of any yet made.   Here is a labyrinth of machinery, for spinning cotton and jute, and various kinds of looms, amongst which is the loom we saw before, making badges and book-marks.   That little island in the sea, has piled up her fabulous wealth, and retains her supremacy very largely, by the wonderful extent of her manufactures, and here we can see a proof of her skill, in almost every department of industry.   Here is a suit made for men, who work in the bottom of the sea.   The body and legs are made from strong canvass india rubber cloth, fastened to a pair of heavy shoes with a sole of lead, about an inch thick, to keep the feet down.   The head piece is made of metal, large enough for the head to turn around to one side, and look out of the glass windows, which you see in front and at each side. This head piece is joined to a plate of iron which sits on the shoulders, and the whole is fastened together, so as to keep the water out, and then air is pumped in the head through that small india rubber tube, which you see is attached. A heavy lead weight is hung upon the diver's breast, so that he will not be thrown backward and lose his balance, but it does not look like a comfortable thing to wear, and it must take a strong and brave man to put it on, and then go down, and down, in the dark water, to work amongst unfortunate wrecks, and perhaps meet with the ghastly bodies of those who went down with them.

But here we come to the display of iron, and machinery, from Pennsylvania; and surely, this noble State need not be ashamed, for in extent and variety, it is a grand exhibition. One thing we must remember, that our prosperity, as a nation, is dependent, to a great extent, on the success of our manufacturing interests. We look, in vain, to find a merely agricultural people, who have become a great and prosperous nation. The clatter of the loom, the whir of the spindle, and the thunders of the forge, must mingle with the buzz of the thrashing machine, and the rattle of the reaper, in order to form a perfect harmony of Plenty and Prosperity.

Did you ever hear of a machine, into which a rod of iron is placed, and horseshoes come out at the rate of sixty per minute, all perfect, with nail holes and creases, and ready to put the corks on for use? Here is just such an one, and it will make all sizes from different sized rods of iron, and it is not a very large machine either, but it is such a mass of ingenious mechanism, that I can not stop to describe just how it works.

Here is a powerful machine for rolling brass. Those large rollers weigh two tons and a half each, and are made of chilled iron, which is harder than steel. They are set quite close together, and will roll a bar of brass into sheets, as smooth and thin as desired. But we catch sight of another crowd, and of course there must be something interesting to be seen. We find they are watching a little saw, as fine as a wire, with which a man is sawing out fanciful chairs, from solid blocks of wood, which are bought as fast as made. The operator can make so true and perfect a cut, that these inlaid figures of men, trees, and animals, have all been cut out, and the pieces of differently colored wood, cut to fit the spaces, have all been made by this saw. It will turn a sharp corner a hundred times easier, than our sharpest financiers, and no figure so fantastic that it can not trace.

I always *supposed*, that tacks were made by machinery, for when a whole paper of tacks can be made, packed, tied up, labeled, and sold for a few cents, still leaving a chance for two or three profits, I thought, of course, not very much time was spent on each tack; but I never knew that each machine would make 450 per minute, of any size, according to the size of the rod used, from a little one, less than a quarter of an inch long, to those an inch and a quarter in length. Here are a whole row of machines, each having a sort of arm, with groove in it, in which the rod of iron is laid, and it is then drawn in and made into tacks, which fall down underneath, like a pouring rain. The machine proper, is only about two feet square.

But we come to another crowd, and we will join them, to see what is going on. There is a beautiful wooden goblet on a stand, the bottom variegated, like a checkerboard, and the sides an alternation of differently colored woods. It is a puzzle to imagine how it can be made, but here is the solution, as we see. Pieces of black walnut and ash, about half an inch square, are fitted and glued together, until a piece of wood as large as the goblet, is made. This is then put in the lathe, and turned, as the turner is now doing, and when oiled and polished in the lathe, makes a very pretty ornament. As we pass along, notice this little machine, which makes, what is called, the Centennial Corkscrew. A small piece of wire is put in, and out it comes, a complete corkscrew, handle and all. Also, notice this very pretty machine, for making corks. The rough corks are put in a little slide, and roll down, and are caught in a little lathe, and a sharp plate, revolving horizontally, and a little chisel, turn them to the proper size, at one revolution, when they are dropped, and roll away, and another is taken up the same way.

Here is a very ingenious machine for sharpening large circular saws. The saw is put in the frame, and an arm, on which an emory wheel revolves very swiftly, moves carefully and precisely, as if endowed with reason, just to the right place on the saw tooth,—for an instant the emery wheel touches the tooth, followed by a stream of sparks, the work is done, and away it goes to the next.

Did you ever pity a man drilling holes in marble and stone, so that it could be broken in the proper places? You have seen them stand, lifting up the drill, which looked like a crowbar, with a blade at the end, turning it a little, and then letting it drop, and so on, through the long tedious days, in the hot sun, or the cold rain. Here is a machine to do the same thing, but it has this advantage, that it works several drills at the same time. See how regularly the drill strikes, every time turning a little, so that it will not strike in the same niche as before. And so the hard, tedious labor of the world is gradually being transferred from man, to machinery; and what a world of aches and pains are thus prevented.

Notice this large case of files, some as fine as the threads of fine linen, and others, like jagged, serpent's teeth. One monster, about nine feet long, and eight inches wide, said to be the largest in the world, is hung up for a sign, and its sides are covered by pictures of ships, docks, buildings, **and** other designs, just to show what can be done.

Here we come to a department devoted to leather, and its manufacture into boots and shoes, and harnesses. Look at the gang of men, making boots, and notice how the labor is divided, so that every man has a certain part to do, and so becomes wonderfully quick and expert, in doing it; so we see that a boot passes through a good many different hands, and operations. First, here is a man who is crimping, or stretching the leather, for the first part of the boot, on a machine; then another sews the seams, as you see; then this one takes them and puts on the sole; another puts on the heel, the next pegs on the sole, the next trims them, and the last works a machine which stretches them, when he rubs out the wrinkles, and makes them smooth, and polishes them, by putting on several preparations, which give them the rich, shining surface, which you see. Here are shoes in gilt and silver, so dainty and exquisite, that they might have been made for Cinderella herself. One of the most ingenious machines, is this, for pegging boots and shoes. The boot is placed on this sort of frame, and placed under the machine. A coil of wood, like a shaving across the grain of the wood, of proper length for pegs, and edges beveled, is on one side, and the machine first makes a hole with an awl, that works up and down, then splits off a piece of the wood from the end of the coil, just the thickness of the peg, and then places it in the hole, and drives it down; and all of these operations are done so swiftly, that the pegs are driven as fast as the clicks of a sewing machine; or, at the wonderful speed of nine hundred pegs a minute.

You have heard of gold and silver quartz mining in which the hard rock is crushed, and the fine particles of silver and gold are separated from the ore; this large machine is for stamping the ore, and will pulverize one hundred and twenty tons a day of the hard flinty rock,which you see lying there, and which does not look as if it was of any value. The mill is about twenty-five feet high, made of a very heavy frame, and the rock is dumped on that platform above, after being broken small enough to be thrown through a hole about five inches in diameter, which lets it down under the immense pestle.

Here is a new machine for dressing stone, which, judging from these chips taken off,which are as large as a man's hand, seems to be a success. The piece of stone passes under two revolving cylinders, each having eighteen cutters fastened to it, in such a way, that they do not strike the stone solidly, but are elastic so that they rebound at every blow. The first dresses it in the rough, the second smoothes it, while the third, with stationary steel knives, gives it a very fine finish. This specimen of very hard rock, showing the successive stages, illustrates exactly how it is done.

Near to it, is a large circular saw, about six feet in diameter, for sawing stone. At the end of each tooth in the saw, a diamond is set, as hard as those used by jewelers, but not as valuable, because they are discolored. A pure diamond of same size would be worth about $200, while these, are worth only $20 or $25.

But here another great gathering has formed, and we find them watching a blind lady working a knitting machine, which, just at present, seems to be out of order; and she is taking out certain parts, arranging them and putting them back, as quickly as any one could; and watch how easily she finds her scissors, cuts a thread, puts them down again on the stand, takes up another article and uses it; in a moment the machine is in proper order again, and she turns the crank and down the stocking comes.

Here is something worth seeing, that shows us that virtue, genius, and a life of genuine service to mankind, will almost consecrate whatever it touches, making their very implements of toil to be sacred things. For instance, here is an old printing press, that intrinsically, is worth nothing, except to burn; an old, stained, oiled, scorched and antiquated affair, of the most primitive fashion, about seven feet high, working with a crank, and requiring a minute or two of severe labor to make one impression; yet if you offered a small fortune for this rickety superannuated article, it would be rejected.

THE MISSISSIPPI BUILDING.

And the secret is this,—Benjamin Franklin, when a journey-man printer in London, worked at this press, and made it immortal; and across the ocean it has been brought, to be sketched and photographed, and written about, and preserved with the most rigid care, to bless the eyes of coming genera-tions. Verily, this is a world of rewards and retributions af-ter all, and this old machine is a capital text to illustrate the doctrine. The poor boy who wearily trudged through the streets of this very city, munching the morsels of bread which he pinched from the loaf under his arm, did not probably have a dream of fame, nor of his future life of usefulness.

But I must not stop to moralize, but we will see what attracts so many on this corner. We find a glass-blower at work making vases of flowers; beautiful birds of different colors, with long sweeping tails, and many other things, curious and ingenious. Notice how he makes that bird's wing of white glass, drawing out the melted glass, and leaving just enough on the body of the bird to fall down as it hardens, and droop just like a bird's wing. It is wonderful how expert these glass-blowers can become. All of these ornaments are made from tubes of glass, which he blows, rolls and shapes into any desired form, and with these sticks of different colored glass. Here is a glass steam-engine which he has made, —balance-wheel, shafts, piston, cylinder,—every part made of glass, and it is working slowly and cautiously as if it was conscious of what it was made.

There is a working model of a stamp mill, from the silver mining regions at Lake Superior, which gives one an excellent idea of those important industries, without taking the time to go to see them. The model is complete, showing the buildings and machinery, and is worked by a small steam-engine, which sets the whole establishment in operation, and the little stamps make a noise that is almost deafening. The ore is run up an elevated track, and dumped down on a platform near the stamps, and when crushed it is carried by a stream of water, over a series of sieves and after many complicated processes, the silver is at last separated from the ore. There were four stamps, and six boilers and engines, and the whole affair is on such a scale of magnitude, as to surprise all who are not familiar with this branch of industry. The buildings are enormous, and the machinery expensive and complicated, and there must be a princely fortune invested in the enterprise.

A very ingenious little apparatus is shown, which is called a drawing machine, and which seemingly, could be made of great assistance in sketching from pictures. A little framework of light pieces of wood is attached to the table, one part of which, is guided to trace the lines on the copy, and that moves another arm in which is inserted a pencil, and

THE ARKANSAS BUILDING. (p. 176.)

corresponding lines are marked by it, on the white paper below. We notice a shingle machine, which is a large horizontal wheel with cutters in it, connected with elaborate machinery and which has a hungry look. Above it is a placard, "Fingers cut off, free" which generous proposition is looked upon with suspicion, and most people are careful to keep at arms length. Another large machine is one for working barrels; but you must not suppose a log of wood is thrust in at one end, and a barrel comes out of the other. Its purpose seems to be particularly, to bring the staves in shape, so that they can be easily hooped, and for this, the staves are set in place; a heavy iron hoop is placed round them; they are then put in the machine, and girthed by strong iron hoops, which are forced down by this wonderful mechanism, until the joints are as close as possible, and thus the process of barrel-making is greatly facilitated.

We have now passed through this wonderful maze of machinery, and noticed the most remarkable objects of interest; and shall long remember these triumphs of man's inventive genius, which do so much to lighten the labor of mankind, and to minister to the wants of our daily lives.

Attractions in The State Buildings.

Many of the States have erected tasteful and elegant
buildings, in which there are registers for the citizens of each
respective State, a reading room, and facilities for writing;
also reception rooms, generally very prettily furnished. Some
of these buildings contain articles of historical interest,
amongst which are many of the most valuable portraits in
oil, in the country, which are worthy one's notice, as well as
limited displays of their respective productions. West Virginia makes a very exhaustive showing of her resources,—a
splendid variety of her native woods, some of which are very
beautiful; for instance, a specimen of black walnut so gnarled
and curled as to resemble the eruption of a volcano, and pop-
lar boards that look as if inlaid with large pearls.

In the Arkansas building is a curious specimen of decayed
wood, petrified, and having the color of rotten wood; also
one of petrified honey, the marks of the honey comb being
plainly visible. Then there is a piece of magnetic iron ore
from Holly Springs, which holds by its magnetic attraction a

THE MISSISSIPPI BUILDING.

nail at an angle of forty-five degrees; and at the end of this, smaller nails are held, one after the other, by the same power, as if all were glued together.   Among a collection of Indian relics, composed of arrow and spear heads, pestles, and earthenware vessels, found in mounds in the State, there lies a barbarous looking iron instrument, very old and rusty, which few would guess was a horse's bit; but we are told that it is an old Spanish bit, and a cruel thing it looks, to put into a horse's mouth, and any one that would do it, must be a stranger to mercy.

Canada has erected a very picturesque, but rude building, made of logs and lumber.   Huge pine logs, set on end form pillars to support the roof, lumber is piled up to make the stairs, and partitions, and an immense pine plank, nine feet wide, and about twenty feet long, makes a spacious table. This plank was cut from a tree 289 feet high, 12 feet in diameter at the ground, and of 603 years growth, as can be ascertained by counting the lines of growth on the end. Bunker Hill monument is 220 feet high.   Let those who have looked from the top of that, imagine a tree 69 feet higher, and you can form some conception of the height of this tree.   The Mississippi building is also built of logs, adorned with rustic work, and draped with those peculiar hanging mosses which grow in their forests, trailing down four or five feet, and giving to it a weird and mournful aspect.

California shows the process of silk growing,—we can see the worms eating the mulberry leaves, and the beautiful cocoons in all stages of growth; and, judging from the specimens here, it would seem that this could be made an important interest in that State. The beauty and variety of the native woods are also finely illustrated by many samples.

The Maryland building contains a striking portrait of Charles Carroll, which belongs to the Historical Society of that State. It shows a fine, dignified, intellectual face, grayish hair, large blue eyes, aquiline nose, and a firm mouth and chin.

We see the banner which Pulaski carried at the head of his legion in the Revolutionary war. It was made by Moravian women, of gilt cloth, and fringed with heavy gold lace, and is about two feet square. It has thirteen stars in the centre, and bears the motto, "Non alius regit."

There is the portrait of Stephen Decatur, the daring naval commander, in full military uniform,—a fine dark face, with a daring look that borders on recklessness.

There is also a portrait of Lord Mansfield, the famous advocate and Lord Chancellor of England, whose career every law student reads with delight. It shows a face almost feminine, so regular and fair and delicate; large eyes, a large nose,

THE CONNECTICUT BUILDING.

broad, but well shaped, and a pleasant beautiful mouth; all set
off like a bright picture in a frame, by his flowing wig, and a
rich robe of ermine.   In the Maine building is an oil painting of "John Alden and Priscilla," by Ernest Longfellow,
the son of the poet.   They are walking on the sea-shore, his,
a smooth-cheeked, youthful, yet thoughtful face, with long
curls and the broad-brimmed hat and wide collar of that time,
hers, a sweet, gentle face, encased in white cap, and turning
to him with expression of supreme content.

In the Connecticut building is a portrait of General Putnam.   It shows a full face, large, round head, prominent
grey eyes, well set nose, and a mouth showing great determination.   Here are also his pistols, which are formidable
looking, indeed, being about a foot in length, the barrels as
large almost as those of a musket.   Near them, is the musket with which he killed the famous wolf,—an ordinary looking weapon with long barrel, and flint lock, and, like the
pistols, looking as if kept more for use than ornament.
There is also his powder horn with an inscription upon it
showing that it was made Nov. 10, 1756, followed by this
poetical effusion :

> When bows, and weighty spears, were used in fight,
> Then nervous limbs Declar'd a man of might.
> But now Gunpowder scorns such strength to own
> And Heroes, not by Limbs, but souls, are shown.

What a furious passion for rhyming they must have had

in those times, when even the powder horn of a gruff old fighter like Putnam, was made the repository for the inevitable verse.   Besides this, the horn bears a plan of the stations from Albany to Lake George, with figures of fortifications, all of this being cut in a distinct manner in large characters.

Near this building there stands an old-fashioned well-curb, with a long sweep swung on a crotch, and pole tied to top, the lower end of the pole being fastened to an "old oaken bucket" such a one as inspired Woodsworth to write the short poem, "The Old Oaken Bucket" which has made him famous.   To how many this will bring back most vividly the scenes of the long ago.

In the Michigan building is a cottonwood log, about ten inches in diameter, which has been cut off by beavers.   It is cut almost square off, and looks as if done by a small gouge from all directions.

In the Wisconsin building, there is an oil portrait of Joseph Crele, who died at Portage City in 1866, aged one hundred and fifty-one years. The portrait shows a face which must have been fine looking when young; white hair, dark eyes, that have a languid look, as if the fires of life were burning low; mouth sunken completely out of shape; brow, cheeks and neck a succession of furrowed wrinkles, looking as if time in his flight, had passed by and forgotten him.

But even such a very old man has been outstripped in the

THE KANSAS AND COLORADO BUILDING.

race of life, for there is also a portrait in oil of Meshoweba, an Indian squaw, who died several years ago in Wisconsin, and who must have been 160 years of age. She had two sons in the Revolutionary army, and was then well advanced in years. She followed our army, doing the cooking for a squad of soldiers, and was present at Yorktown at the surrender of Cornwallis. For many years she was carefully provided for by the Indians of Wisconsin. The picture shows her wrapped in a white blanket, with head bare; an old, old face, having the Indian features; broad cheek bones, straggling, coarse gray hair, but eyes black and clear; her face and neck look like leather, and as if moulded into wrinkles; and yet, many squaws are as old looking as she. Of the three millions living at the time of the Revolution, she was selected as the sole survivor—the solitary link between the early colonial days and our generation. The brave, the beautiful, and the great were all doomed to be swept away by the pitiless tide of time, and this old squaw alone, destined to outlive them all.

But of all the State buildings, that occupied jointly by Kansas and Colorado, deserves the highest praise, and enlists far more attention than any other. These enterprising young States have an Exposition by themselves, which will repay one for hours of careful observation. On one side is represented by means of painted oilcloth a rocky ledge covered with patches of vegetation here and there, down which a little foam-

ing cascade pours on the rocks below.   On this rocky ledge
are fixed splendid stuffed specimens of all the native animals
and birds in the two States; buffaloes, bears, antelope, the
wolf, fox, prairie dog, rabbit, racoon, opossum, and others, as
well as wild turkeys, geese, ducks, prairie hens, cranes, owls,
quails, snipe, and many other varieties, all fixed in a natural
position, and producing a striking effect, especially as you
learn that all of these were shot and stuffed by a small, quiet
looking, middle aged lady, who is with them, and has deservedly
earned all the attention she receives.   There are buffalo
robes, on which are pictures of different colors made by the
squaws,—some of squaws with papooses, on horseback,—tomahawks, bows, arrows, quivers and knives, and various designs,
all more skillfully done than one would expect.   There is a
very extensive exhibit of silver ores from Colorado, one piece
of which, weighing about a ton and a half, and not looking
half so rich as many shining boulders in some old pasture,
contains silver worth $736.   Another specimen contains
$1000 worth of silver to the ton, but to unpractised eyes, it
looks no richer than another sample which yields $200 to the
ton.   There is a specimen of selected gold ore, which yields at
the rate of $25000 per ton, and it does not look particularly
rich either.   They have a gold button, about one and a half
inches in diameter, and perhaps half an inch thick in middle,
which is worth $60, and was taken from one pound of ore.

THE NEW JERSEY BUILDING.

A button of silver containing about as much as a silver dollar, was extracted from one ounce of ore.   In other specimens, gold as large as peas is seen cropping out of the rock; but most of the gold exists in the form of fine dust, which is extracted by skillful processes, and elaborate and powerful machinery.

On the side of a smooth piece of rock, about two feet long, a fern leaf is traced as delicately and distinctly, as if drawn in India ink.   There are mammoth bulbs of morning glories, about two feet long, and one foot in diameter, and samples of grains, which can scarcely be surpassed, all bearing witness to the wonderful fertility of the soil.   Mr. G. Hopper, a native of the West, is an individual well known, by reputation, in public circles, but comparatively few have seen him. For those who are anxious to gratify their curiosity, there are several corpses, preserved in alcohol.   They are about two and a half inches long, and three quarters of an inch in width, and are as savage and formidable in aspect, as can well be imagined. On the wall, there hangs the coat of Kit Carson, the famous Indian scout.   The outside is made of dressed buckskin, with fringe of the same material, and the body is embroidered in certain places, with blue and pink silk, in fanciful designs; the collar is of black velvet, plain, black buttons; the inside is of strong, coarse cloth, making a very warm, heavy garment. Those scouts and mountaineers, although isolated from the

world, do not lose quite all their vanity, for the love of ornament in dress is seen cropping out, even there.

Some enterprising, and kind individual, anxious to serve the
next generation, is exhibiting a century clock, which he
claims, when once wound up, will run, and keep good time,
till the next Centennial. The weight weighs 600 pounds, and
during the century, will fall six feet and four inches. It is
about eight feet high, and two feet square, which is quite
small for the amount of work it has to do.

The earth is full of mysteries. For instance, here is a petrified fish, looking very much like a brook trout, which was
found four hundred feet below the surface of the earth, in a
shaft of a mine. How did it come there? A large mass of
metal which looks like solid gold, is called "fool's gold,"
because it is nothing but pyrites of iron, and is worthless.
Some magnificent specimens of agate are shown, which are
supposed to be petrifications of wood, and also, rock crystals,
which are very beautiful. A curiosity is seen in a piece of
solid silver quartz rock, just as it came from the earth, which
seems to have the masonic sign, of square and compass, upon
it, in several places. A small bunch of faded flowers is shown,
which were plucked by one hand, while the other gathered a
snow ball. This was on one of the mountains in Colorado,
near the snow line, and illustrates the contrasts and peculiar-
ities of that wonderful country. An interesting picture

THE PENNSYLVANIA BUILDING.

hangs on the wall, of mountains, trees, foliage, and cattle, made entirely from a collection of mosses and barks. There is a fine stuffed Rocky Mountain sheep, which has strong horns, and is as large as a good sized calf, and is well adapted for climbing and leaping. He has hair, however, instead of wool, and seems to belong to the deer family, rather than to that of the sheep. Excellent specimens of coal are also exhibited, as well as iron ore, and, of course, many other articles which have not been mentioned, but we have endeavored to notice the most remarkable in the collection.

The Beautiful Algerian.

Many people imagine that the houri of the Arabian nights and the Oriental beauties of Byron were pure creations of fancy, and have no counter-type in actual life. All such should see the Algerian lady, in the bazaar for the sale of goods from Algiers; and they would have reason to think, that those characters, were not altogether creations of the fancy. Imagine a fair, white complexion, a beautifully shaped head eyes of lustrous blackness, long dark eyelashes, and eyelids that must have been penciled in the Eastern manner, so striking is the effect. A nose of perfect symmetry, and a mouth small, but well shaped, lips like ruby, and when opened disclosing teeth perfectly regular, and white as ivory,—a chin in perfect harmony with the face, and jet black hair forming a glorious contrast with the fair brow, and white neck,—and you may form some conception of the Oriental type of beauty. On her head she wears a rich robe, which is like the setting to a jewel; and as a part of the usual costume of her country, is worn a richly embroidered velvet jacket. But while her beauty is surpassingly great, and to our eyes, of a type almost startling in its strangeness and perfection, yet there is something wanting which we see in thousands of plain faces, and in ordinary characters in the great world around us. There is

lacking that delicate and womanly kindliness of soul, that
denotes a refined nature and a noble heart, and which in ten
thousand happy homes, sheds a light more glorious, than lustrous orbs of Oriental lovliness.   Here is beauty that would
fill the artist with rapture, and would remind him of the classic
features of the old Grecian masters, and yet the nameless grace
and urbanity that distinguishes the true lady was lacking.
She is continuallv surrounded by a host of admirers with
whom she does a flourishing trade in the vending of her photo-
graphs, and the numerous knick knacks for sale.   A boy about
fifteen years of age, seemingly a member of the family, and
actiug as salesman, has also the same inheritance of personal
beauty.   His face is a rich olive color, and his eyes are
black as night, and like flashing gems.   The phlegmatic pro-
prietor of the establishment is on the contrary, a blonde gentleman of the extremest type,—fair, ruddy complexion, blue
eyes and light hair, and beard, and a perfect contrast to the
lady we have described.   He wears an immense turban,
a highly colored jacket, and loose trousers, and seems to be
wide-awake in the management of his business.   Among their
wares they have perfumed beads, purporting to be made from
berries obtained in the vicinity of Lebanon; pipes of Eastern
design and profusely ornamented; silk handkerchiefs of exquisite texture and design, and richly embroidered cloths and
articles of apparel, and many other articles of ornament very
attractive to the eye.

The Marvels of Agricultural Hall.

Ceres, the protectress of agriculture, was one of the greatest divinities in ancient mythology, but it is very doubtful whether ever before, she has been honored by such a tribute as we see in these vast acres covered with the choicest products of earth, agricultural machinery, and manufactured articles of domestic use.

From this imposing display of the earth's fruitfulness, and man's ingenuity, let us gather a few trophies. The nations, represented by separate departments, are Great Britain and Ireland, Canada, New Zealand, South Australia, France, Germany, Austria, Hungary, Portugal and her colonies, Italy,, Venezuela, Japan, Liberia, Brazil, Denmark, Sweden, Argentine Republic, Spain, Russia ; and among the States of our own country, Iowa, Ohio, Michigan, Oregon, and Washington Territory, have made fine exhibits of their agricultural resources. It would be tedious to enumerate all the varied productions which each of these countries have contributed, but some of the most striking we will notice as we pass along.

1776
AGRICULTURAL BUILDING.
1876.

In the department of Great Britain and Ireland we see fine specimens of wool, candy, straw bee-hives, shell work, vases of flowers, mill machinery, terra cotta work, large steam engines on wheels, for farm work; also agricultural implements, and many other articles covering a large space.

Canada has a splendid display of modern farm machinery, horse rakes, drills, threshing machines, plows, fanning mills, reapers, and many others, and is not far behind our own country in the design and finish of these implements. There is also an excellent display of the cereals, of great variety, and finest quality.

In France, one of the most noticeable features, is a large assortment of balances and scales, for weighing, and they look extremely rude and clumsy, when compared with those in general use in this country. There are also large assortments of wines and brandies, and machinery for their manufacture.

Germany, and Austria and Hungary, do not make as fine displays as might be expected from the immense resources of those countries. Both Germany and Austria have displayed very conspicuously, on towers built for the purpose, large numbers of mowing scythes, which are from three to five inches wide, and are clumsy and burdensome indeed, compared with those exhibited by American manufacturers. They have large exhibits of wines, cigars, wool, and small grains.

Portugal, and her colonies on the African coast, have a department containing many articles of interest. Here is an immense tusk of ivory, about six feet long, and six inches in diameter; assortments of coffee; platters and dishes made of wicker work, and fine collection of precious woods; a rude loom about three feet square, made and used by native Africans, and which will weave cloth about the width and quality of our coarse towels. Then there is a whole museum of weapons of warfare, used by the savage Africans,—murderous looking spears with long steel blades, some with three prongs; shields made of wicker work, bows, arrows, and clubs, and also a large variety of battle-axes, daggers and swords, which look as if they had done murderous service for many long years. A wax figure, life size, so fierce in aspect, and life-like in appearance, as to be almost startling at first view, gives one an excellent idea of the costume of those African tribes. It is very scant and simple, consisting of a sash of white cloth over one shoulder, a girdle of same around the loins, a belt around the waist, in which is stuck a dangerous looking dagger; sandals on the feet, and an immense red turban on the head.

These colonies are rich in choicest woods, of which there are numerous samples, some of which are susceptible of a wonderful polish.

In the Italian department we notice oranges, lemons, macaroni, rice, nuts, candied fruits, ores, leather, soap in huge blocks, jute, wines, and some fine lithographic stones.   One of the best ways to ascertain whether a country is progressive is to examine the style of plows used, and here we are agreeably disappointed to find good plows and harrows of modern patterns, which is certainly a cheering sign of promise for the future, for if the great interests of agriculture are neglected, there is not much hope of a permanent prosperity

The little republic of Liberia exhibits unhulled coffee as large as hazel nuts, flax, coal, iron ores, dyewoods, cereals of fine quality, and an immense tusk of ivory.   A piece of native ore is shown which has been forged without smelting, just as it was taken from the ground, and contains 94 per cent. of iron.   A native African loom is a curiosity, showing how in nearly all barbarous tribes, some sort of a loom seems to be invented.   This is only about a foot square, and weighs only one pound and fourteen ounces, and yet it has woven cloth of quite good quality with red and dark stripes, looking almost as well as some of our coarse ginghams.

The department representing Venezuela is also very interesting.   Here, too, is a marvelous array of the most beautiful ornamental woods, showing a richness of variety, which is astonishing, and well illustrates the boundless natural resources of those tropical climes.   Strange to say, there are superb boquets of wax flowers, showing perfectly the rich coloring, and the massive luxuriance of the floral sisterhood in that sunny land. There is also beautiful embroidery of richly colored feathers, which are suggestive of the brilliantly plumed songsters, which vie in lavishness of color, with the flowers and leaves amongst which they dwell.

Here is a work of exquisite taste and wondrous patience, which interests us at once. It is a strikingly natural portrait of Washington; the angel of Liberty crowning him with a wreath; on one side is a bust of General Bolivar, on the other of Lincoln, both resting on pedestals, and we are truly amazed when we learn that all this, so natural, and harmonious in coloring, is made of human hair. This admirable piece of work is set in a rich gilt frame, and is not only a specimen of consummate skill, but is also a beautiful tribute to our country and the memory of the immortal Washington.

It is a matter of surprise that Russsia is so far advanced in farm machinery. But here are steam-engines on trucks, for farm work, threshing machines, containing substantially the modern improvements; fanning-mills, reapers with self-raking attachments, and other machinery, finished in the most attractive manner, and showing that they are fully awake on this subject. There is also, a splendid display of small grains, jute, and of the different varieties of wood. There are also wax figures, showing the dress of the people, which is merely an immense fur sack, reaching almost to the feet, with hood attached, the bottom of the robe and the trimmings being of darker fur, making a very comfortable and picturesque costume, which looks as if it might, render a Russian winter, tolerable. There are shoes made of cloth about half an inch thick which looks as if pressed together, and warm enough for any climate.

There are also very excellent specimens of wool, some of which show a clip not less than five inches long, and of exceeding fineness.

The Empire of Brazil has done herself great credit in this building, as in others, by the richness and variety of her exhibits. One of the most noticeable things, is a palace of cotton, which is a circular building of wood; covered with masses of loose white cotton, the top of the walls ornamented with tall plumes of this material, giving to it a very pleasing and picturesque aspect. In the inside is a monument of coffees, the whole calling particular attention to two great productions of that country. The display of woods is magnificent, and the wonderful resources of the famous Brazilian forests are well attested here. One piece of wood is smoothed and highly polished, and the grain looks like leaves and blossoms, so exquisite are its fantastic curvings. To most people, it must be a new revelation in the matter of ornamental wood. Here is also india rubber as it comes from the tree, jute, tobacco, cigars, rope, leopard skins, leather, and well built plows, which indicate an advanced system of agriculture. The display of small grains is also excellent.

Holland has, amongst other things, a fine showing of corks, jute, cheese, beeswax, bent wood and cables. There is also a model of a Dutch fishing galley, so wide as to be almost like a tub. It has one mast, and illustrates the character of its builders to go slowly, and keep right side up. A great curiosity is a section of a wooden fence, about six feet square, which is a part of a hedge formed by a shrub, called "Merveilleuse," which, when planted about six inches apart and the saplings interlaced, grows together, the branches joining each other, and becoming knotty and gnarly, thus making an impenetrable fence, looking like a huge sieve.

Denmark displays fine specimens of small grains, butter, and bottled liquors and cordials.

In the Swedish department are plows of good design and workmanship, a large variety of small grains, cured fish, leather, and many models of their boats and vessels, which indicate a thorough knowledge of boat and ship building.

The Argentine Republic shows to fine advantage, the resources of that country; one of the most surprising sights, is the great variety of precious woods, adapted for the most costly and beautiful ornamental work. Then there are excellent specimens of furs, wool, the small grains, raisins, nuts, sugar, cheese, hides and silks.

The chief display of Norway consists of all kinds of dried fish, nets, and fishing tackle, boats, and fishing smacks.

In regard to our own country, it would require a volume to describe the machinery exhibited. There are plows, which almost belong to the department of art, silver plated, their wood work of mahogany, or rosewood, polished as if for a parlor, and so graceful in design, that it would seem sport to turn a furrow. Here are mowers and reapers, of the same exquisite workmanship, and of every pattern; some with long, curved arms, look like swan's necks and heads, which grasp the bundles of grain like things of life, and bind them tightly with wire. To enumerate all, would be to give a catalogue of nearly all the best labor-saving farm machinery of the age. It covers the floor by the acre, and the countless cogs, wheels, pulleys, sickles, bars, reels, and other paraphernalia in motion, make a pandemonium of noise and bluster, that would almost drive a nervous person into hysterics.

Some of the States have separate departments, which are very creditable, amongst which, is that of Iowa, which has glass jars, about six feet high, showing a sample of the soil from most of the counties in that State, to a depth of six feet, and in most of them, it shows a rich loam to that depth. There is, also, a very fine collection of specimens of the woods of Iowa, which, in variety and beauty, must create a general surprise, for the State has not been noted in that respect. There is a beautiful inlaid table, of exquisite workmanship, made of 3,983 pieces of the different woods of Iowa, which sets them out to great advantage, and which required six months of dilligent labor to make. There is, also, a very fine display of fruit, which must convince the most skeptical, that the western prairies are adapted to the cultivation of the choicest varieties of apples, pears, plums, quinces, grapes, and many other fruits. Here are apples, immense in size, red and golden, which fairly make one's mouth water. There are also, specimens of corn, and the small grains, which attest, better than advertisements, the fertility of this noble State.

Ohio also exhibits small grains, corn, wool, and other products, while Michigan has chiefly devoted her energies to setting forth the richness and extent of her pine lumber interests, by showing splendid samples of her lumber and logs, in boards and plank, some of which are very large.

Oregon has a very interesting department, which illustrates the fertility of the soil, on the Pacific coast.

The productiveness of the soil is truly marvelous. Here is a clump of 140 stalks of wheat, by actual count, full grown and each one having a perfect head of wheat, all of which grew from one kernel, and there is another much larger which must have at least 250 stalks perfectly grown and head-

AN OLD MILL IN AGRICULTURAL HALL.

ed like the other, making a clump of stalks about six inches
in diameter, which grew also from one grain. So that it is
necessary to sow only about one quarter as much seed as is
ordinarily done in the Middle or Western States.   The
samples of all kinds of grain, are very fine, as is also their
wool, and different varieties of woods.

There is a tract of country in Oregon, about thirty miles
long, and eight wide, on which manna, or honey dew falls,
like the dew.   It coats the grass and leaves like varnish, and
is so sweet, that the bees make honey from it.   There is a
branch shown here, on which it has fallen, and it looks like
the white sugar, or saccharine matter we see on raisins, and
seems to be in sufficient quantities to be gathered.

California is also represented here by a fine exhibit of ores,
shells, and a collections of stuffed birds, and small animals of
that wonderful region, which would delight the heart of a
naturalist.   What must be the size of a monster whose teeth
were seven inches long and three inches broad, and yet that
is the dimension of a mastodon's tooth we notice.   Another
very curious looking object is a rough stone called a "totum,"
which is carved like a bird, and carried by the Iudians of the
Pacific coast, on the prows of their canoes, probably to drive
off the bad spirits, or for some other reason suggested by
their superstitions. A piece of petrified wood, is also a curiosity,—the grain of the wood being distinctly preserved, and

yet like flint.　Here, too, is the celebrated grape vine of Santa Barbara, Californa, of such immense size, and so prolific in bearing.　It is about sixteen inches in diameter at the base, and runs up about seven feet, when it spreads out and is supported by a frame, which is flat like a ceiling.　The tradition of the vine, has extended near and far; and as near as we can gather is as follows, and might be called:

The Romance of a Grape-Vine.

About seventy years ago, a Spanish family lived near one of the numerous missions, which were flourishing at that time, in the country which now constitutes California, (but which was then under Spanish rule,) who were blessed with the presence of a beautiful daughter.　She was famous for her charms and accomplishments throughout all that region, and had no lack of suitors who sought her hand. Amongst those who threw themselves at her feet, she looked with favor on one—a handsome young man, who captured her heart by his manly bearing, and sterling qualities, and who was fitted in every way to be a desirable companion for her, except that he was poor.　The parents were ambitious, and wished to procure a rich husband for her, and so looked upon the young man with coldness and repulsion. He asked their consent to the hand of the daughter, was refused and driven away, and commanded never again to see her face.

In order to break the attachment between the lovers, the parents decided they would suddenly remove to another mission, one hundred miles away, trusting that time, distance, and new associations, would soon cause the daughter to forget her lover. She managed to apprise him of this, and they had a clandestine meeting, in which he confided to her, that friendly Indians had communicated to him the knowledge of a gold mine, which he was determined to find, and that he would return with great riches, and thus remove the obstacle, to their union, and so pledging mutual constancy they separated; but, before he departed, he presented her with a grape cutting for a riding whip, to carry on the intended journey, as a reminder of him. The removal was soon made, but the grape-vine was carefully preserved by the beautiful betrothed, as a memento of her absent lover, and in a favorite spot, near the new home, she planted it, and under her watchful care it grew with wonderful vigor. After a time, the parents found what they considered a suitable husband for their daughter; he was old and ugly to be sure, but these slight objections were overshadowed by the fact that he was rich—at least, so thought the parents—at any rate, their eyes were so feasted, and their minds were so exhilerated by the display of the glittering gold, of their prespective son-in-law, that they were completely blinded to every other consideration— moreover the rich suitor was thoroughly infatuated with the charming maiden. She protested and resisted as long as possible, but at length her stern and unrelenting father so exerted his authority, that she was compelled to succumb. Under many pretexts, she succeeded in delaying the nuptials for two years, trusting that some good fortune would interpose, and especially that her absent lover would realize his dreams of wealth, and return before the dreaded day that would soon be set for the imposing marriage ceremony. At length the day was fixed, and the evening before, she went to her loved grape-vine, crushed by unutterable anguish and despair, wishing that death would terminate her misery, but while thus prostrated by grief, she heard a rustling of leaves and light footsteps, and in an instant appeared the welcome form of her lover, who had returned, with all his visions of affluence realized. With joy they sought the sordid parents, and soon convinced them of his good fortune, and they willingly acquiesced in the choice of their daughter, now that their objection was removed. The marriage was consummated, and as the years rolled by, they brought with them all the happiness and prosperity that could bless a large and well ordered household. But after many years, reverses came, and their wealth vanished, as it ever may, and they were reduced to proverty.   The grape-vine in the meantime, have been growing luxuriantly, and every year becoming more prolific; until now, when proverty came, its yield was so great and valuable that it supplied the simple wants of the family, and saved them from want until the days of prosperity came again.   The couple whose lives had seen so much of romance, passed away, but the old grape-vine cherished its life, and every year grew, and strengthened, until it reached its present proportions.   And with such romantic associations it has become the most famous grape-vine on the continent.

One of the conspicuous objects of interest, is a plow said to have been made by Daniel Webster, in 1837. It resembles him, in being built on a large scale, for it is thirteen feet long, having a beam nine feet in length.   It has a wooden mould board, with plates of iron nailed on it, and is constructed with coulter and wheel in front, and was evidently made to plow new land full of roots and stumps.   It must have been a favorite with him, for this is what he said of it: "When I have hold of the handles of my big plow, with four yoke of oxen to pull it through, and hear the roots crack, and see the stumps go under the furrow out of sight, and observe the clear, mellowed surface of the plowed land, I feel more enthusiasm over my achievement, than comes over my encounters of public life in Washington."   Hear this, ye thousands who are holding the plow handles in disgust, and

are longing to leave them for the whirl and excitement of
city life, the dangerous experiment of commercial business,
or the wranglings and disappointments of a political career—
hear this, from the most magnificent intellect, and grandest
orator of this continent, before whom senates were moved
at the majesty of his genius, and admiring thousands ready
to do him homage. If a man of such powers, with such suc-
cesses, found the rewards so barren, what can you expect with
your limited powers and meagre opportunities? That old
plow will preach many a sermon, as it stands there, rusty and
weather beaten—its occupation forever gone, except to remain as an honored tribute to the nobility of well-directed
labor.

Our Schools and Some Others

Most of the States have provided educational departments
in the main building, which are together in a row, one opening through to the other. These are filled with libraries,
maps, charts, extensive collections of apparatus, text-books,
cases of specimens in mineralogy and natural history; many
having valuable cabinets from college collections. Tables are
also provided, on which are the examination papers of the
schools in each State, particularly of the larger towns and
cities, and often of small but enterprising villages, which papers are finely bound together in handsome volumes, inviting
the visitor to examine their contents. There are often bound
collections of photographic views of the school-buildings, so
that by a careful examination of all these, one may
determine the comparative rank of each State in this direction. These departments are, generally, exceedingly tastily
furnished, and provided with large books for the names of
teachers and visitors from the respective States, in which
they are expected to register. As we pass through them,
now looking at the reports of a high school, then perhaps, a

ladies' seminary, then at a common school, and see the often fine penmanship, the admirable drawings, and the intelligent and appropriate answers to the questions presented, we can not but feel a just pride in our glorious system of free education.

The State of Pennsylvania has a large octagon building, all by herself, which is full of interesting articles. There are large collections of brooms, mats, brushes, cushions, clothing, and many other articles, made by the blind; beautiful pencil and crayon drawings, specimens of penmanship, extensive libraries, the most approved school furniture, a section representing an old school-house, with pegs on wall, old box stove, rude oak, desks, and the indispensable strap hanging up, which was indispensable to the old fashioned pedagogue.

Sweden has sent over a full-sized building, the same as those adopted by her for her public schools, and every part was brought here, ready to be put together on the grounds. It is made of pine, something like a Swiss *chalet*, with very wide and overhanging eaves; the sides of grooved squared timber laid one on another, and the whole building constructed, as the gentleman in charge informs us, without any nails or spikes. Inside the walls are wainscotted, and the ceiling made of matched boards, all of which are oiled. There are double front doors which are arched, made out of strong plank, with heavy iron hinges. We enter a hall, on the left of which, is the main room, with a neat teacher's room off at one side, supplied with a compact teacher's library; while to the right of the hall, is a room for cabinets, and for recitations. The building is intended for about one hundred pupils, with two or three teachers. The main building is about twenty feet wide and fifty in length, in the front on a platform is a neat teacher's desk, and behind it, is a map rack; on one side is a cabinet in mineralogy and entomology, on the other sides are maps, globes, philosophic and astronomical apparatus. On the walls are charts illustrating natural history, geology, and physical geography, and various maps. There is a curious map made on a sort of black board, with wooden pegs stuck in holes to mark the cities and towns, so that when the pupil is asked to point out a city, he sticks the peg in the hole which marks the place. The seats and desks are single, and are similar to the most approved patterns in our schools, and are made of light wood oiled and varnished. The desk is provided with inkstand in front, a little frame to lean the open books against, and a rack for the slate. The top of the desk raises up, and underneath is a place for books. There is a frame provided for the feet to rest upon, and everything seems to have been done for convenience and comfort. On one side of the room is a singular sheet-iron stove which is enamelled with a white surface, is about three feet wide and two feet deep, and extends from the floor about ten feet high, the top ornamented with a neat cornice, and the whole having a pleasing appearance. The walls are hung with numerous colored charts; illustrating all departments of natural history, and there are several cases of stuffed birds, fishes and dried mosses. The external appearance of the building is decidedly picturesque and attractive.

Norway also occupies a space with the furniture of a modern school-room, and it certainly indicates the most advanced ideas in educational matters. The seats and desks are of modern style, teacher's desk, and map rack in front, with maps and globe,—the whole seeming to be much the same as the best school-furniture of our own land.

Belgium has sent a model also of a school-building, such as is adopted by the government for public schools. It is built of wood, and the inside is neatly constructed with colored sections, so as to afford a more pleasing variety to the eye than a plain wall. The seats and desks are of wood, and made for two pupils, and are comfortable and substantial. In the front of the room is the teacher's desk, and a map rack. There is a striking similarity between the furniture and appointments of all these school-buildings, showing that the interest in education is becoming more and more general, and that an improvement adopted in one country is soon caught up by others, and readily adopted.

The Turkish Cafe.

We have all read of the Turkish cafe, where the luxury loving Turks smoke long pipes, and drink the purest Mocha. This fanciful looking structure, built in the form of an octagon, with such a queer roof is one, and supposed to be built after the genuine Turkish fashion; suppose we visit it. In the centre of the room are tables and chairs; around the outside are luxurious cushioned sofas, which have fancifully figured coverings, and have a decidedly hospitable aspect. The curtains are of highly colored, heavy material, and give to the room a sort of Oriental air. Behind the counter, on one side, sits a Turkish woman, acting as cashier of the establishment, wearing a gayly embroidered velvet garment —her magnificent black hair, dressed in our modern style. She has a splendid figure, and a sensitive, refined face, as white as many brunettes of the Anglo-Saxon race. We take a seat on the sofa, and a stalwart young Turk, dressed in a gay, red jacket, immense trousers, and turban, approaches to take our order. We glance at his handsome face, black mustache, broad shoulders, and vigorous frame, and instantly decide that the Turks are not more effeminate than

some other people; and then order coffee. Our host repeats
the order to the presiding genius of the back room, with a
stentorian voice, loud enough. to awaken the seven sleepers;
and in a moment, brings a little cup about the size of an egg
cup, placed in a metal holder. In a few moments the smoking mocha appears in a small. brass ladle, which holds about
three tablespoons full of coffee. It is already sweetened, and
so we proceed to taste the beverage. We find it to be thick,
like cream, the grounds as fine as flour, the flavor delicious,
and we sip the rich amber, which acts on the system at once
as a tonic, and drives away fatigue. There is about a tea-
spoonful of grounds in the bottom, which the Turks take
with the coffee, but which we leave in the cup. Near us,
groups are smoking the famous long Turkish pipes, with
stems about six feet long, and seem determined to enjoy solid
comfort from the experiment. Customers come in rapidly,
the dissonant, thundering orders are given at short intervals;
parties and groups are continually looking in, and passing
through, to see the novel spectacle, and the lady at the counter, is a continual target for numberless glances from bright
eyes; but the Turks are not to be abashed by smiles or
laughter, but mind their business, well contented, so long as
they can do a flourishing trade. I cannot see but that the
Oriental mind is as keenly alive to the pleasure of gathering
dollars, as the most acquisitive of any other race.

HORTICULTURAL HALL.

Horticultural Hall.

This building is charmingly situated, quite large, and one of the most beautiful on the grounds. At a little distance, a guano company, to show the fertilizing properties of their preparation, have handsomely decorated a large expanse of the lawn, by magnificent collections of tropical plants, which seem to grow in all the vigor and luxuriance of their native climes. If we ascend the gallery of the building, we shall see these with all their alternations of shades, and also the perfectly kept flower beds which are fairly radiant with bright colors, and extend in pleasing variety, one after another in the distance. If we look within the building, we see a succession of pretty arches, extending down the sides, which are made of red, white and black, brick-laid alternately, and gaily painted designs above, which give it a tasty and pleasing appearance. Beneath, we see the luxuriant masses of tropical vegetation, with their wonderful depth of coloring, the beautiful fountains, and the glittering chandeliers, and we are charmed with the beauties of the scene before us. Many of the plants and flowers are of great size, and rare varieties, and would well repay a lover of Flora, with a taste for botany, to spend much time in their study. But as an exhibition, this department does not compare in variety and extent, with many other departments of the Exposition; and so, with this brief glance we will pass on.

The Castellani Collection of Ancient Curiosities.

Signor Castellani is an Italian gentleman of great wealth, who has devoted himself·to the study of archæological pursuits and spent a liberal share of his fortune in obtaining this collection of valuable and interesting articles, which give us a glimpse of the people and customs that were in existence thousands of years ago. We are told on good authority, that this collection is valued at $400,000, and surely it must have taken years of patient labor, animated by a quenchless enthusiasm, and assisted by an almost exhaustless purse, to have brought together all of those varied treasures. Those who think that we live in an age of greater artistic excellence than any which have preceded it, should withhold their judgment until they see these beautiful pieces of statuary, many of which are, and will be, models of perfection in art. Here for instance, is a bust of an unknown Roman lady, which is dark and stained by age and exposure, but how the perfect Roman profile and the delicate, regular features are brought out, in all their beauty. An original bust of Sappho, the celebrated Grecian poetess, shows a fine, strong face, large eyes and aquiline nose, well formed mouth, and flowing hair bound back in a graceful coil. Here is a statue of Perseus, supposed to be the work of Phidias, the greatest of Greek sculptors. It has been sadly marred by some vandal hands, for the nose is broken off, and it is stained in many places, but still shows traces of its former beauty.   A bust of the Emperor Augustus, who is said to have found Rome in brick and left it in marble, represents a magnificent head of a beardless young man, very much unlike what we would expect from the selfish and crafty character described in history. It shows a large brain, a refined and expressive face, the mouth in particular, indicative of a delicate and sensitive nature.

Here are statues of Cupid and Psyche, of the school of Praxiteles, another of the great Grecian sculptors. They are heads of the finest mould, the faces being of the most perfect Grecian type of beauty. There is a head of Alexander the Great, showing his head leaning sideways, as history informs us that it did. This is also badly disfigured—the nose being broken off. It shows a strong, full face with regular features, expressive of sternness and determination.

Here is the head of the Apollo, the Greek god of song and beauty. The nose of this is also broken, and yet sufficient is left of the perfect features—the large eyes, the well formed mouth, the beardless face, and the luxuriant hair thrown back, to reveal the glorious symmetry of this noble work.

We see a full length statue of " Bacchus," the god of wine, amongst the Grecian divinities.   It represents a fine regular face, very long hair and beard, and a flowing robe thrown over one shoulder, and hanging gracefully to the feet.   This piece of statuary was found near Naples in 1875.   Next, we notice the bust of Euripides, the celebrated tragic poet.   The face is not particularly remarkable in expression—having a retreating forehead, overhanging eyebrows, sunken eyes, a large nose, and a heavy beard and mustache.   Here, also, is the head of the Emperor Tiberius, which was found in Naples in 1437. The features are strongly Roman,—a large round head, Roman nose, thin lips, and protruding chin, the face denoting a curious compound of intellect, decision and sensuality.

There is a statue of a Roman matron,—a beautiful face, with regular features, a smiling expression, and her beauty adorned by a loose mantle of rich pattern.

One of the most remarkable pieces of statuary is that of The Spinario, which represents a naked boy seated on a rock, and taking a splint from his foot.   The position of the body, the natural appearance of the flesh and muscles, the expression of the face,—all are wonderful, and make this one of the choicest masterpieces of art of all the ages.

Here are a collection of bronze articles of the sixth century, which were found in tombs near Rome. There are balances, with scale, and a beautiful female head as a weight,—toilet caskets about the size of a large ladies work-box, of greenish color, covered with beautiful chasings,—scenes from Roman mythology, warriors with plumed helmets, and armed with short swords and shields,—imaginary winged figures, stately matrons, war horses, and many other fanciful designs. We can inspect here, a Roman lady's toilet set,—of course it appears at a disadvantage as it has not been used for about twelve hundred years, and since then we might suppose the fashions had changed, but yet, you may see a rouge pot with the rouge still in it, showing that this art has survived empires, dynasties and civilizations;—you may see also combs, tweezers, hand mirrors, much the shape of those used to-day, but of highly polished metal instead of glass;—buttons, a sponge, and a great many other articles for toilet uses, the purpose of which it is difficult to guess. There is also a specimen of a small cup with a cherub carved upon it, of ivory carving, which is very ingeniously executed.

Here is a collection of ornaments which belonged to the early Christians, who were compelled to take refuge in the catacombs of Rome, to escape the terrible persecutions of the infuriated heathen rulers, and these articles were found in those dreary recesses. They must have had many supersti-

tions, for here are many charms and amulets, of various patterns; also, brass rings, of many designs, ornaments, rude
glass and copper medals, with inscriptions. There are, also,
coins from a very remote time, some that are merely pieces
of metal, used before the art of engraving was applied to
money; others of brass and iron, with the portrait of the
monarch on them, in whose reign they were made. Here is
a wonderful collection of finger rings, from the earliest period
of Tyre, to the sixteenth century. Some are of gold, and are
in the shape of a serpent, coiled around the finger. There
are immense ones, of gold or brass, about two inches long,
and very large precious stones in the back, and with inscriptions inside and out. A large one, made of stone, has a group
of statuary on four sides. There are necklaces, large ear-
rings, and other articles of personal adornment, made of
brass, in the bronze age, which are quite rude in appearance;
and ornaments in amber, made at about the same period;
amongst them, rude statuary, and sketches of human faces.
Here are ornaments of glass and silver, set in gold, which
go back to the time of the Phœnician kings, and which were
taken from the cemeteries of Etruria. Also, a very old
Egyptian image in ivory, and a necklace with pieces of glass
beaded upon it. The glass is very opaque, and nothing like
the clear, transparent crystal, of to-day. There are, also,
gold ornaments taken from the Etrurian cemeteries, which

were made seven hundred years before Christ; one of an image of a lion in gold, another a carving in ivory, and a plate which looks like heavy gold leaf, and, apparently, had designs pressed upon it, by being stamped in moulds.

. Here is a collection of Egyptian ornaments, which were made away back in the reign of the Macedonian kings. They consist of rings, necklaces, ear-rings, bracelets and a large brooch; showing that the articles of female adornment were much the same then as now.

A collection of Greek ornaments is shown, which were made in the days of Demosthenes, Plato, and Aristotle. We notice colored porcelain, jars, vases,—one of transparent glass, —large gold ear-rings, with small ivory birds and beasts attached, and tiny carved human figures, about half an inch long, and yet very perfect. But one of the most wonderful collections, is that of a case of cameos cut in almost every kind of precious stones,—amethysts, sards, emeralds, garnets, and others, which go back to the days of Nineveh and Persepolis, and show the progress of cameo cutting, from those remote periods, to modern times. Here are the lineaments of Egyptian princes, and Roman Emperors,—others from Phœnicia, Etruria and Greece, with the busts of reigning monarchs, —mythological deities, master-pieces of classic art cut upon them in the most exquisite manner. Here is one for instance, less than half an inch square, on which is cut the figure of a bard, with flowing hair, playing on his harp; every part brought out in the most spirited manner, and executed with consummate skill.   There are probably about one hundred of these gems and cameos, in this collection; and they constitute one of the most interesting art studies that can be found. Here we can see for ourselves, the work of the cunning artificers of Egypt at a very remote period, of Nineveh, and Phœnicia, of Greece and Rome.   What must have been the civilizations, which could have produced such perfect models, such glorious conceptions, and such perfection of art. We notice also a collection of ornaments worn in the time of Charlemagne in the eight and ninth centuries, consisting of a cross, a brass necklace, brooch, ear-rings, rings and pins, which look rough and coarse to our eyes, but which are quite elaborately ornamented.   There are also some military ornaments, which were worn by the Crusaders, consisting of several buckles, a colored plate for a belt, with a design of four shields, and another of four dragons.   Specimens of porcelain made by the Arabs in Sicily, from the twelfth to the sixteenth centuries, and colored with fantastic blue and drab figures, are very interesting and unique; as also are several immense volumes of illuminated missals on vellum about two feet square, which were made by monks in Italian abbeys in the fifteenth century.   They are wonderfully beautiful with their rich gilt, and exquisite colored illuminations and pictures.

You have heard of the lost art in glazing porcelain, by a process known in the middle ages,—here is a case filled with articles made by that unknown method,—and as the setting sun throws a flood of light upon it, it becomes radiant with a molten glory of purple and gold, as if the expiring orb of day would reveal to our eyes, for a few fleeting moments, the departed glory of the illustrious past.

Pre-historic Races and Relics.

There is abundant material here to engage the attention of archæologists for weeks. Models in clay are to be seen in the Government Building, of the houses of the " cave dwellers," found in Arizona, which are supposed to have been deserted more than five hundred years, and to have been inhabited by a race of the Aztec tribe, now extinct. They were made of high walls of solid stone masonry, and were built by the side of cliffs, or ledges of rock, the wall of rock forming one side, and were entered through square windows, or openings, which were high above the ground, and were reached by ladders, which they could draw in after them. From these models,we should judge these walls to be from fifty to seventy feet in height. A smaller collection of relics is to be seen, which were found in the vicinity of these caves. They consist wholly of earthenware, which is coarse in character, some black and white and roughly glazed. We notice a dipper, bowls, a water jar, and fragments of other pottery. One pitcher, about six inches in height, is glazed and colored blue and black. There is also a model of the ruins of an ancient tower, or circular building, found in southwestern Colorado. It was built of brick, with an inner and an outer circle of heavy wall, and the space between, divided into regular compartments. It seems to have been built in a good workman-like manner, and would indicate that the builders were a people of a high degree of intelligence.

In an annex of the main building, are exhibited many collections and relics of great value. Amongst them is said to be the largest specimen of copper in the world, an immense mass weighing 5720 lbs., which was found in Isle Royal, Lake Superior, in 1875, in an old mine pit of the stone age, about sixteen feet deep. It shows the marks of the stone hammers of that age, and is of a greenish color; it has a rough surface and is in the shape of a heart with the bottom round.

From a mound near Kalamazoo, Mich., were taken an interesting collection of copper implements, which are here exhibited, amongst which, is a needle about two inches long, an awl and a file, a spade about seven inches long and three inches wide, made, for a handle; knives, one of whose blades is nine inches long, another six inches, an axe of good shape, but no eye in it, and apparently made to be fastened to the handle by thongs or wire.

In another Michigan collection of relics from the stone age, are arrows of black and white flints, queer red and black pipes, stone hammers, pestles of many sizes, a very curious etching marked and painted on stone, representing a naked figure bound to a tree as if to be burned, while near by two Indians, with high head dresses of feathers, are struggling together as if in deadly conflict. At the right are seen two other trees, and a black canoe, apparently on the ground. The ground is colored green, and some faint coloring is seen in other parts of the picture, but it is very dim. The figures are quite well drawn, and their positions are natural.

In a collection from Ohio, is seen a curious looking object marked a "copper sandal," which is shaped as if to fit the sole of the foot,—also pots, bottles, drinking vessels, dishes, jars, all of coarse earthenware,—stone hammers, arrows, idols, round stone balls, and a very valuable collection of copper articles, amongst which are arrows, hatchets, a dagger with handle, a chisel, a large axe, and a plate of copper about four inches square. Perhaps the most curious is a piece of carved stone called the "Cincinnati tablet," which was found in a large mound in that city. The mound was about twenty feet high, and seventy-five feet wide at the base. The tablet is about six inches wide, four inches high, and half an inch thick. There is a border on the outside, and within it characters are graven as regular as those in a Chinese book, and, at a casual glance look very much the same. In this collection there is also, a white stone tomahawk with an eye for a handle; a pebble with the head of a deer skillfully cut upon it,—a lizard cut in medallion on a piece of black stone, and a white pipe with an Indian figure cut upon it.

Here is a curious pipe, with a human face carved on the bowl, a shank about five inches long, on which are three naked figures kneeling as in adoration,—the first more prostrate than the others, and all symmetrically shaped, and the position natural,—also there is seen a figure-head of a man attached to the rude body of a beast, which was found eleven feet below the surface of the ground, whilst digging a well in Ohio.

The largest collection in the world of copper materials from the pre-historic races, is from Wisconsin; and is truly astonishing. Here we see what is apparently a set of surgical instruments,—small knives, one and two inches in length, axes of different sizes, large knives with curved blades, and some smooth and sharp spear heads, some with long sharp points, and others wide and short, and made for both wooden and metal handles,—a fierce looking instrument, something like a dirk knife, with blade about nine inches long. The collection is of remarkable interest, and must contain about one hundred implements of copper alone. We have thus noticed some of the remains of the "cave dwellers." and "mound-builders," the two pre-historic races, whose people once had a home on this continent, but which have been swept away, leaving only these fragments

behind, to denote that they ever had an existence.   As we
see these articles of such varied shapes, designed for so many
uses, indicating races, which though not civilized, yet must
have possessed a considerable degree of intelligence,—the
mind is filled with questionings, which these specimens of
their workmanship merely suggest, but which furnish no
answer.   When, and how, did these races reach this continent,
and people it in such numbers, as to leave behind them, these
articles of their manufacture, in localities so widely separate
from each other.   From whence did they come, and to what
branch of the human family did they belong?   We may well
say with Hamlet:

> " There are more things in heaven and earth, Horatio,
> Than are dreamed of in your philosophy."

Odds and Ends; Here and There.

The Spanish Building.

This is quite a large building, and contains very much to interest and instruct. Here is a collection of coins from remote ages down to the present time. Some of the oldest ones are of silver, and are very large, being about three inches in diameter. A collection of native weapons from the Phillipine Islands is shown, having bows and arrows made of bamboo cane with metal heads, and quivers of woven cane, and also spears of many patterns, often very tastefully made. A beautiful piece of shell work is seen, representing the figure of a worshipper with clasped hands before a cross, which has wreaths hanging over it, most of which is made from shells. A curious coat of arms is made from brass plates, joined together by rings between them; and near it, are murderous looking swords, some of whose blades are serpentine with handles of various shapes, some almost like needles, some long and some very short, and a battle axe inlaid with gold. On one side lies a mahogany log, about two feet square, and

THE SPANISH BUILDING.

twenty feet long; one side of which is polished, showing its beautiful color and grain. We may see here bamboo canes from eight inches in diameter down. There are wax models, life size, showing the uniform and weapons of the Spanish soldiers. For instance, here is a lancer, with an iron cap, with lance about ten feet long, dressed in light blue coat and pants, also a cavalry-man, dressed in jacket, very gayly embroidered with yellow, and blue pants; he, also, carrying a long lance. There, are, also small brass field pieces, models of pontoon bridges, mounted artillery fortications, aqueducts, and other public works.

When we see the large newspapers of to-day, with their immense amount of news, we seldom think of what they used to be. Here is a specimen of the " New England Journal" printed in 1728,—a very small sheet, and printed on a coarse looking paper. The editor thus begins to extol his wares for the commendable purpose of increasing his subscription list. " There are measures concerting, for rendering this paper more universally esteemed and useful, in which 'tis hoped the publick will be gratified, and by which those gentlemen who desire to be improved in history, philosophy, poetry, etc., will be greatly advantaged."

In Cook, Jenkins & Co.'s ticket office are a collection of curiosities from Egypt, amongst which is a mummy of an Egyptian princess or priestess, who lived three thousand years ago, in the days of the Pharaohs. The case or coffin is made of wood, and covered with Egyptian characters, supposed to be prayers for the dead. The body is black and shrivelled, and was bandaged with coarse cloth. At the head of the coffin is a portrait, supposed to be that of the occupant, which is in colors, and represents a face of pleasing expression, and strong Egyptian features. There are also a collection of Egyptian swords, some of them are curved almost like sickles—slender spears, about eighteen feet long, fierce looking daggers, and shields made of hide, carved with designs, and so hard as to resist any blow of spear or sword.

Here is a building containing a model of a silver quartz mill from Chili, of surprising capacity, and it plainly indicates that silver mining in that country, must be an important interest. There are six large hoppers in which the ore is dumped, and in each of these, there turns two immense metal wheels which crush it to powder, a stream of water running in and mixing with it. It is then transferred into vats, where it is dried by evaporation, then put into revolving barrels where it remains for about eight hours, and it is subject to an elaborate process to be separated by the use of quicksilver. It is a vast enterprise, and gives us a glimpse of the capital and resources of that country, which we never had before. Near it, is a model of a pneumatic tube, designed to supersede railroads, for transmitting mail matter and freight. It is a long air tight pipe, smooth inside, from one end of which the air is pumped, and a ball, fitting closely, and in which the freight is placed, is started at the other, and driven through at a great velocity by the pressure of the atmosphere. It is claimed that a velocity of one hundred miles per hour, can be attained by these balls, and that this system is practical on roads many miles long, the balls to be from seven to nine feet in diameter.

There is a pile driver here, worked by gunpowder, and which has driven a pile through this very hard clay, seventy-two feet down, averaging thirteen inches at a blow. There are two very heavy iron hammers, working in a groove in a frame, one above the other. The lower one which strikes the pile has a hole on the top about eighteen inches deep, in which an iron bar from the other enters. When used, the upper one is raised about ten feet, a cartridge with percussion surface is thrown in the hole in the lower hammer, which explodes when the bar in the upper one falls upon it, and the explosion both drives the pile down, and sends the upper hammer up about ten feet, where it is caught by machinery, and held until the process is repeated, which is very rapid. This far supercedes the old method by driving by the mere weight of the hammer.

The French have a separate building, which is extremely interesting to those who have a liking to examine great public improvements; and it affords a very good opportunity to observe the enterprise and ingenuity of that people in works of this kind.   Here are charts, drawings and models of their greatest public works, such as bridges, roads, aqueducts, railroads, the methods of supplying towns, cities and canals with water, internal navigation, light-houses, fortifications, harbors, and many other things that show the wonderful system of public improvements, which has been carried forward in France, and which is a convincing proof of their material prosperity.

We find an exhibition here by a Humane Society, which is a sickening evidence of the depraving of human brutes, in the fiendish cruelty they exercise toward other brutes.   Here for instance, is shown the stuffed body of a bull-dog after a fight, his head a raw, bleeding mass of wounds, his mouth torn open, one foot bitten to pieces, his eyes almost torn out,—a sight which sickens us to see; also stuffed specimens of cocks after they have fought, which are equally repulsive; and we naturally wonder, how it is possible for the human heart to attain such loathsome depravity, as to take delight in such disgusting spectacles.   Here are pictures of miserable horses, which have been found at work with great raw sores under the collars, and other parts of the harness, and clubs are shown, with long spikes in the end, which were used by drivers in driving swine and cattle.   So long as men are cruel

THE JAPANESE BUILDING.

to beasts, they will be cruel to each other; and these Humane Societies should be aided by every one, who feels any desire to see humanity and public morals on a higher plane.

"Old Abe," the famous war eagle from Wisconsin, who was carried by a regiment through battles and campaigns, is doing his part to make the Exposition a success, for he sits patiently all the day long, eyeing and turning his head at the curious faces continually around him, thus making his fame more enduring.

Studies from the Art Gallery.

Soul in Colors.

Some men become famous by writing a single poem; but we see before us the portrait of a man whose fame rests largely upon a single line of poetry, more than all else. It is Bishop Berkeley, the author of the familiar line that has glittered like a gem in so many orations, and rounded off so many periods, in daring flights of eloquence—

"Westward the star of empire takes its way."

It is a most beautiful face,—full, fresh and blooming; a mouth expressive of good humor; a well-set nose; darkly arched eyebrows, and kindly dark eyes, all set off to fine advantage by a graceful wig, which gives a dignified courtliness to the figure, which nothing else can supply.

We will next examine a most interesting picture, entitled "Milton and his daughters." The blind old poet is sitting in his arm chair, with his cane in one hand and the other raised towards his head, as if he were struggling to find expression for his sublime fancy,—his face showing in a wonderful man-

THE ART GALLERY.

ner, the working of the mind, which is wholly absorbed in deep thought. His youngest daughter sits towards him, as if to encourage him by her near presence,—the lamp shedding its mellow light on her exquisite profile, rich dark hair and white neck, with charming effect; while the elder sister sits in the shadow of the lamp, and is busily engaged as amanuensis, and is recording for posterity, the welcome words as they are dictated by the grand old bard.

A very expressive picture is entitled "The marriage of the Covenanters." The scene is in a Scottish glen, and on an eminence in the distance, a sentinel is seen to apprise the company of danger. The heroic bride and groom stand in the foreground, waiting for the service, and the pastor is looking seriously at the groom, as if to divine whether he had strength of will sufficiently to warrant this important step, in such troublous times. The old church clerk has his book in his hand, and his inkstand on a rock, ready to make the record. At a distance a disputatious old covenanter is arguing some mooted point, and has his finger on his bible, as if to clinch his argument. On the other side a sturdy warrior, clad in armor, looks gloomily, as if thinking the future too dark for such a step, while near him, some maidens are peering, curious to see the ceremony. The picture is large and worthy of study.

Who does not remember " Eva St. Clair," in "Uncle Tom's

Cabin," one of the purest creations in the whole realm of fic-
tions, and which lingers in the memory as an angel of light
and beauty. Here is a beautiful picture in the Italian gallery,
representing her as described in that exquisite passage in the
story—sitting in the garden, reading her bible, a face dreamy
and thoughtful, as if wondering at the glories of the New
Jerusalem, described in her favorite book of Revelations. Her
features are beautiful; but not so much as the soul which shines
through them, and gives her face an expression of angelic
purity.

We will next notice a very fine picture in the German gallery, called "Lady Jane Grey's triumph over Bishop Gardiner,"
which is worthy of the most careful study. It represents
Lady Jane in the dungeon, seated, with Bible before her,
clothed in a robe of scarlet velvet, with the high white collars of that day. She sits erect, and her sweet, and perfect
face is expressive of the strongest resolution. At her side is
a table, and on it, the pen and ink with which she has refused to sign the articles of recantation. Between her and the
door, stands the Bishop, clothed in his robe of purple and
ermine, and skull-cap—one hand on a chair, the other
clutching the roll she has refused to sign, wearing a stern
countenance. His eyes flash with rage and indignation, and
he looks at her with a vindictive expression, which she returns with a calm but resolute gaze. Behind her chair stands

her faithful attendant, her hands clasped in grief and despair, but looking intently through her tears at the Bishop, to see if there are no signs of relenting in his countenance. No one can see this striking conception of the subject, without admiring more than ever before, the sweet disposition and dauntless courage of the noble, but unfortunate heroine.

In the French gallery is a massive picture, which is one of the most noticeable in the entire collection. The subject is "Rispah protecting the bodies of her sons," and the story is told in the Bible, in 2 Sam., xx."

The picture is a scene draped with the shadows of night. As far as the eye can penetrate the gloom, are seen desolate rocks, dangerous seams and frightful chasms. In the distance, ominous birds of prey are approaching. In the foreground is a rude frame, on which the bodies of the young men are hung, their spears, shields and swords placed above them. The bodies are naked, except that some have girdles, necklace and helmet, and in the dim light they have a most pallid and ghastly appearance. Rispah stands in front of the gibbet, a magnificient figure of the strongest type of Jewish beauty; her large black eyes angrily flashing as she stands, with club in one hand, and the other upraised, to ward off an immense eagle, which, with talons and beak extended, is endeavoring to reach the bodies. She is clothed in a rich yellow robe, with a heavy figured purple sash around her

body, and a purple robe hanging loosely from her head;
and in the conflict with the fierce bird of prey, she stands
erect, defiant, and resolute—her mother's grief finding expression in the heroic protection of the mangled bodies of her
beautiful sons.   In the distance are smoke and clouds and
murky vapors. The scene is one of wonderful power, and
one which the memory will not willingly let slip.

Studies of the Beautiful.

Italy is celebrated as the land of art and song. Where the
sky is so blue, the shadows so soft, the landscapes so charming, it is not strange, that an atmosphere of art is created,
and that men are tempted to copy with the chisel and brush,
the varied charms which surround them. In this bewildering collection of exquisite statuary, it will be impossible to
notice all that well deserve study, but let us examine a few
of the most admirable, both as to the nature of the subject,
and to the most perfect skill of the artist. Here is a beautiful piece of work called "After School," which will bring
back to thousands, the golden memories of that opening page,
that illuminated frontispiece of life—the school days of girl-
hood. It is a full length figure of a school-girl, in that golden

period of life, when the charming simplicity of childhood, is blended with the grace and dignity of coming womanhood. She has ball in hand, ready for a joyous game, and is carrying a garland of flowers. Her beautiful face is no longer made somber by the shadows of study, but it is smiling, joyous—as if inviting and welcoming every recreation, which the restful moments can bring. Notice the graceful, natural poise of the body, suggestive of the poetry of motion; the delicately moulded throat, the hair thrown back, as if revelling in its freedom; and the whole is a study of airy grace, and winsome light-heartedness, which the eye dwells upon with fondness, and the memory recalls with infinite delight.

But we turn to two figures, of mother and child, entitled, "Beggars," and wonder whether in Italy there is such a redundance of beauty and gracefulness, that even the beggers are fit to sit as models for the most ambitious artist. Beauty is a queen that cannot be concealed by rags, or by any outward condition of life; and so in the sweet expressive face and comely form of this beggar woman, she reigns triumphant, over poverty and adverse fate. The garment is old and tattered, but how gracefully it sweeps down fold after fold,—the spirit may be crushed and the mien, submissive and cringing, but how expressive the downcast eyes and the patient and appealing cast of countenance, all forming a type of beauty which makes poverty an adornment, and sorrow a garb of comeliness. And how the heart is touched by this boy beggar, with the head of a cherub, whose cheeks are not yet sunken by hunger nor hardened by crime. He stands forward appealing for alms, with face downcast; but nature is too exuberant, his curiosity to see the gift, is too powerful to resist, and his beautiful eyes are cautiously peering under the rich lashes, while his face is faintly illumined by the repressed roguery of his child nature, with which he is richly endowed, but which he has already learned to conceal. How these white chiselings become, indeed, "sermons in stone," and recall to our inner nature, the infinitely varying phases of human experience, not only of the outward life, but also of the heart, and inner consciousness.

Here is a beautiful piece of statuary, which shows in a very marked manner, the wonderful possibilities of the sculptor's art, which is called "The Veiled Girl." The face is represented as closely veiled, and yet the large expressive eyes and drooping lids, the aquiline nose, and finely shaped mouth are plainly discernible, as if the veil were half transparent. It seems impossible that you are gazing at a solid block of marble, for the illusion is so complete, that you feel tempted to draw the veil aside, and see in all their perfection, the charming, half disclosed features.

But we will turn from these triumphs of art from sunny Italy, and notice a few from artists of our own country.

Miss Vinnie Ream has been the subject of much newspaper comment, and to read the editorials and criticisms in our political journals, one would suppose that she was more entitled to distinction as a lobbyist, than as an artist. But here is her work, standing side by side with that of others, to be judged by its own merits, and asking no measured praise in its favor. The beautiful statue, called " The West," is one of her productions, and is truly a charming conception. It is a full length female figure, holding a compass in one arm, and a surveyor's chain in the other. She has a classical face, luxuriant hair flowing back, and is standing on a sheaf of wheat, with arrows and broken bow at her feet. There is something so airy and sprightly about it, as to be almost an exhiliration. The *pose* is extremely graceful, and the expression of the face looking at something beyond in the distance, is the history of the great West in a look. To almost every one, the West is a subject full of never failing interest and pride. It is suggestive of heroic endeavor, and its richest rewards,—of wildernesses made to blossom, of fortunes repaired, of an asylum for the poor. It is the land of golden hopes, great achievement, and romantic exploits. All of this is suggested by this beautiful figure, so eloquent in expression.

Here is another statue by the same artist, a full length figure of " Miriam," the prophetess. To me, this woman, so full of song and praise as to seize a timbrel, and to lead in a dance and chorus of joy and thanksgiving, before the assembled hosts of Israel, has always been one of the richest female characters in the Bible, and worthy of the most glowing conception of the artist. Here we have a beautiful face, full of enthusiasm, a graceful figure draped in flowing robes, and leaning forward as if to lead the procession, while in her hand the timbrel is uplifted, as if she were almost delirious with the joy of leading the rapturous song of triumph.

Another most exquisite creation of genius, is a statue representing that famous beauty of antiquity, so celebrated in song and story, Helen of Troy. It is an inspiration of beauty, showing the most delicate and regular features, a magnificent figure, an admirable *pose*, and glorious hair, wavy and flowing, and is justly entitled to be ranked as one of the most admirable pieces of statuary in the collection. But let us turn for a short time, to this most gorgeous painting, in the Austrian gallery, entitled, "Venice paying homage to Caterina Cornaro." It is about thirty-six feet long, and fourteen feet high, and in brilliancy of coloring, richness of design, and exquisite finish, it is a marvel of perfection. Cornaro was the wife of a king, and on the death of her husband, presented her kingdom to the Republic of Venice, and in grateful acknowledgment of her generosity, the citizens, once a year, brought these gifts to do her homage, and this is the subject of the artist. Cornaro is attired in the richest

embroidered robe of purple and gold, and is seated on an
elevated position, on a chair of state, which is overhung with
a canopy of scarlet drapery. She has an exquisitely beautiful
face and figure, and is seated with perfect grace and dignity, and
extends her hand most graciously to those who present their
offerings. At her side, stands a cardinal in scarlet robes, and
easy dignified posture. Before her a beautiful woman is pre-
senting a casket of jewels, another an offering of flowers and
fruit. Further back, a venerable sage, with bent form and
long white beard, presses forward to do her homage, while
behind follows a water-carrier with a finely ornamented vase
on her head,—a fine, stately, erect figure, with rich olive skin,
and magnificent profile. Further back is another female, with
face of most bewildering beauty, and near her, an Ethiopian,
covered with a rich, red velvet robe, is hastening to present a
casket of pearls, while above, in an elevated position,
stands the troubadour, with long black hair, and dark, dreamy
face, leaning gracefully against a column, dressed in red cap
and purple robe, and thrumming his guitar. It is a picture
of wonderful brilliancy—of tropical gorgeousness. In richness
and luxuriance of design and coloring, it is perhaps the most
remarkable of any work in the entire collection.

A beautiful conception is a picture entitled, "Day," in the
Norwegian gallery. It represents a spirited war horse bounding through the clouds, on which is seated a beautiful boy, with

fair, open face, dressed in blue robe and red cloak, who is holding up a blazing torch with outstretched hand. The steed is so spirited, the face so fair, the coloring so harmonious, the conception so poetic, that one can scarce see it without having the imagination quickened.

But one of the sweetest and most suggestive works of art, is a piece of Italian statuary, entitled, " Faith." It represents a closely veiled female figure, but yet the head is erect, and the manner triumphant, as if she had the most unshaken confidence in the way before her, and implicit faith in the future. It is impossible to describe in words, the wonderful beauty of this sweet and delicate conception,—the very impersonation of loving trust and unquestioning faith. It looks as if you could pierce through the veil, and see the expression of triumph underneath.

Glimpses of the Horrible.

A Spanish picture, entitled, " A Duel in the Seventeenth Century," represents two cavaliers, with strong Spanish features, who are engaged in a duel, with swords. One has received a fatal wound, dropped his sword, and staggered against the wall for support. The expression of agony on his sallow face, and his apparent exhaustion are fearful in the extreme.

The Pope sent from Rome, a wonderful picture in tapestry, "The Martyrdom of St. Agnes," in which the martyr stands on a pile of burning fagots, her face upraised to Heaven in prayer. The colors on this are so finely worked, that at a short distance it might be taken for an oil painting.

"Prometheus Bound," is a massive English picture, in which the magnificent form of Prometheus, is chained to the rock, the muscles of his body showing his agony, but his face resolute and defiant. The vultures are about him, ready to tear out his vitals, but his spirit does not quail.

"A Scene at the Destruction of Pompeii," is a graphic representation of the terrible catastrophe. A group have taken refuge in a cellar. A magnificient beauty has fallen unconsciously into the lap of her mother, her jewel case beside her, the jewels half thrown out—while the mother regards her with distraction. A matron is bringing in her naked boy, who hides his face from the sight. A beautiful maiden, terror stricken, looks on the scene with horror, and rests in the arms of her slave, who leans back as if resigned to her fate. The lurid light from burning lava streams in at the entrance, and warns them of their doom.

English history is blotted with the record of many dark deeds, but one of the most horrible in its atrocity, was the blinding of Prince Arthur. In the German gallery, this is made the subject of a picture, which we will notice. The scene is in the prince's bed-chamber. Arthur is a beautful boy, dressed in blue attire, and having long auburn curls, and stands with his hands thrown up to the old grey-headed jailer, as if with confidence and trustfulness. The jailer, with the heart of a fiend, holds the boy's head with his left hand, and with the right is covertly seizing behind him, a pair of pincers holding a piece of red-hot iron, with which to sear the eyeballs of the innocent and unsuspecting boy. The hot iron is being taken from a vessel of burning charcoal, which is brought by two swarthy black-smiths, who shrink back, as if unable to bear the horrid sight. And, so is shown, one of the most cruel and fiendish crimes which history records.

Another horrible picture is one entitled, " The Inquisition,' representing a victim undergoing torture, stretched on his back, with arms and feet bound, while fire is applied to the soles of his feet. The agony expressed in the countenance of the poor writhing victim, and the diabolical fiendishness of the inhuman inquisitors, are alike shown, and cause a shud-der at such a fearful exhibition of "man's inhumanity to man."

In the Belgium gallery is a grand painting entitled, "Chris-tian Martyrs in reign of Diocletian." The scene is in a dun-geon, with massive stone walls, in which, on a pallet of straw, on the stone floor, lies a young Christian martyr asleep. He is naked, except a girdle about his loins; in his hand he grasps the cross, as if unwilling to be separated from it, even in his dreams. He lies with his face towards us—a beautiful, youthful face, with a look, peaceful and serene, as if fanned by the wings of angels,—the finely cut mouth, half open, as if with the simplicity of childhood, while the relaxed muscles and every position of his magnificent form show a slumber, serene, natural, and refreshing. The keeper is just throwing back the immense doors of thick timbers; and through a chink of the door, a ray of sunlight falls across the body of the sleeper, like a benediction of mercy, to illumine his few brief moments of life, with a foretaste of heavenly glory.

The partly opened door reveals the immense amphitheatre, with gallery above gallery, crowded with eager spectators, waiting impatiently for the bloody and uneven combat; while on one side, the mouth and claws of a ravenous tiger are seen, impatiently awaiting his feast of human gore.

The Humorous in Art.

Humor does not seem to be a favorite quality with artists, for they generally aim at subjects which contain elements of sublimity, esthetic beauty, or historic interest; and consequently it is not strange that we find but comparatively few pictures of a humorous character. Yet there are sufficient to arouse one's sense of the ludicrous in a high degree, and these are probably enough. The most remarkable is one of Landseers', called "The Travelled Monkey." An old monkey has returned from his travels to the secluded glen, where his tribe dwells, and is surrounded by his wondering acquaintances, to whom he is relating his adventures. He is dressed in the height of fashion; a flowing wig, velvet cap, scarlet coat, and the accessories of a fashionable dandy, including all the airs and attitudes of the most conceited fop. He carries his gloves in his left hand, and with his right, jauntily holds the butt of his riding whip to his mouth, so that it shall surely be noticed. At a distance, one of his curious friends, who has stolen his snuff box, is in great grief, having opened the box, and in inspecting the contents, got the snuff into his nose, mouth and eyes, and is sneezing and rubbing his eyes with most astonishing vigor; while another, of like curious disposition, has torn off a piece of gold lace from the traveler's coat tail, and is picking it to pieces, with great diligence, and appears to receive much satisfaction from the operation. An old monkey is about to shake hands with the distinguished tourist, but looks intently, as if wondering whether he is not mistaken, and holding up his left hand in speechless astonishment. In the far distance are seen the elegant mansions and towering spires of the busy world, and fashionable life, from which the illustrious traveler has

returned. The picture is a rich satire on some of the frailties of mankind.

Another exquisite bit of humor is called "Nobody was born
a Master." A roguish boy is shaving his grandfather, and has
sliced off a large piece of his face. The wrathy old gentleman
is ascertaining the extent of the damage by a mirror, while
the young rogue stands off, out of reach, with razor in hand;
but there is a merry twinkle in his eye which he cannot re-
strain, and it requires his utmost effort to look demure.

"The Contented Hermit," is another picture, rich with humor. The old hermit has one of those jolly faces that will have
their way, and as he sits on a rock, fast asleep, with his head
against a tree, and his violin in one hand and bow in the
other, he looks the very picture of content, notwithstanding
his coarse robe, bare breast, and the grinning skull beside
him.

Another strange picture represents Louis XI., of France,
sick, and gypsies have brought into the palace educated
pigs, dressed in costume, to dance before him, and thus en-
tertain him. While one is dancing, another is being trained
at a short distance away. What would be thought now, of a
powerful monarch of an enlightened country, if he required
such diversions.

"Chesterfield's Ante-room," is a picture that will provoke a
smile. In the gorgeously furnished room, sits Dr. Johnson,

who has apparently been admitted by the servants, and been waiting some time for the appearance of the accomplished Chesterfield. Liveried servants and pretty maids are cracking their jokes at the gruff and burly philosopher, while he sits fuming with impatience, and beside himself with vexation, at being so shockingly snubbed by his noble patron.

"A Whisky Ring" represents a melancholy instance of the woes of the lower animals, if they aspire to imitate the example of men. A bottle of whisky had been left unopened by some careless teetotaler, and a boisterous company of mice, out on a spree, and determined to have a good time, have upset it, and are in all the stages of delirious exaltation. One, more enterprising than the rest, has already indulged so much that he lies stretched out, supposed to be supremely happy, and entirely indifferent to the obligations of existence; another is rapidly hastening to the same condition, but has still self-consciousness enough left to kick one hind leg and to raise his head, and gaze despairingly at his feeble movements, and his total inability to help himself; another, who is almost human in his indomitable dissipation, is already powerless on his back, but still licking the mouth of the bottle, determined to die game, while his more cautious neighbor, of a more philosophic turn of mind, is peering into the mouth of the bottle, determined to satisfy his inquiring disposition by property preliminary investigation, before com-

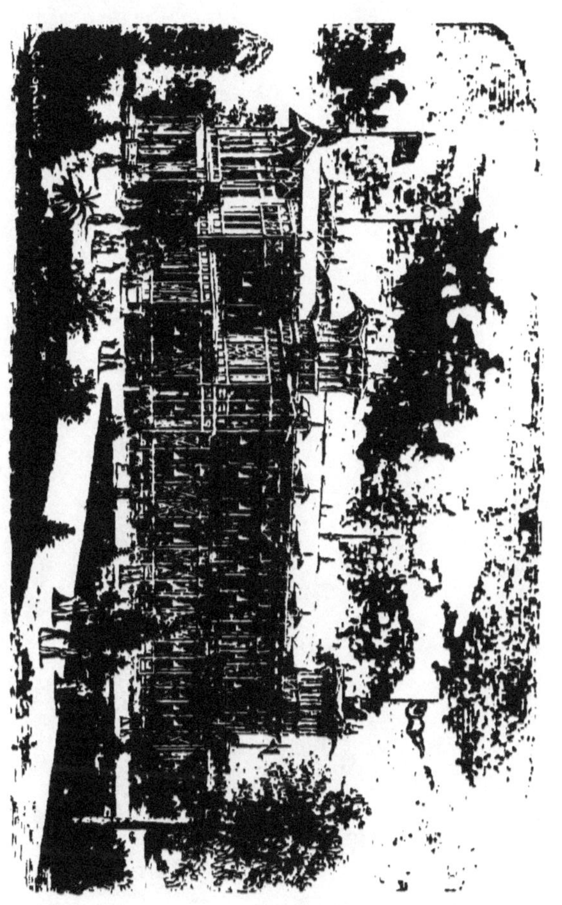

THE JUDGES HALL

mitting himself to the forgetfulness of intoxication. The picture is not only a burlesque, but a sermon.

Character in Chiselings.

Here is a wonderful statute of "Media," who in ancient mythology, was a princess famous for her skill in sorcery. She became the wife of Jason, and helped him to obtain the celebrated golden fleece, but was afterwards deserted by him, and in revenge, murdered their two children. The statue represents her as if in meditation before the bloody, and unnatural crime was committed,—holding the dagger in her right hand, the left upraised as if nervous and irresolute,— her head downcast as if in deep thought, her beautiful face expressive of intense anger, and yet doubting whether to gratify her revenge. Her wavy hair is thrown back, and bound in place; her flowing robes fall in the most graceful folds, and the position of the body is singularly easy and natural. Altogether it is a triumph of art, and is the work of W. W. Story, the famous American sculptor, now at Rome.

Miss Edmonia Lewis, the colored artist, has a full length figure in marble, entitled "Cleopatra in Death," which attracts much attention. The figure is reclining in a royal chair, the body thrown back, and the head resting on one side, as if tired of life.   The face has strongly marked features, and wears a wearied, desperate expression.   In her right hand she holds the asp, which is writhing in her grasp, but her disgust and weariness of life is so intense, that she is indifferent to its poison and fangs, and does not even notice its angry struggles.   Her face represents a cruel, sensuous, and restless nature, without any satisfaction in the past, or hope for the future, and determined to cast away the precious boon of life, as if it were a bauble not worth the having, and thus quench the pangs of remorse and disappointment.

But here is a colossal bust that would attract notice anywhere.   Shaggy hair and beard, a noble brow, large full eyes, a large well shaped nose, a firm and decided mouth, and an expression of strength of will, that would resist the power of worlds sooner than succumb; it is such a face and head as we might suppose would belong to one of earth's noblest heroes.   And in the light of history, who shall say it did not, for it belonged to a man, who though misguided in judgment, sacrificed his life for a principle, and was actuated by the most sincere convictions of duty,—John Brown.

We next notice a fine statue of Humboldt, the great German traveler and savan.   A massive brow, regular features, kindly eyes, a large, well set nose, projecting eyebrows, a face of thoughtfulness and intellectual power, with the broad cheek bones peculiar to the German type of countenance. Hair long and curly, and thrown back from the brow. A piece of work that should be a sermon to thousands who will see it, whose lives are listless and aimless, for it shows the lineaments of one of the world's noblest workers.

The old hero Garibaldi, whose life has been spent in the cause of Italian liberty, is one of the favorites of the sculptors —several of his statues being here by different artists. Long, straight, coarse hair and mustache, hollow cheeks, sunken eyes, and a large nose, he looks like the strong, rugged character as he is, as grim and unyielding in his purposes, when fully aroused as inexorable fate, yet with a nature so impressible and fervid, as to glow with the fiercest heat of enthusiasm, and so tender as to melt with sympathy, for those in distress.

A beautiful statue of Dante, shows a tall, graceful, dignified figure, with flowing robes, reaching to the feet, holding in his hand a roll pointing to the ground. A massive brow, large, expressive eyes that have a look of sadness in them, as if still seeing the terrors of the Inferno;—and so penetrating,—as if they would pierce you through and through; thin, sunken cheeks like those of a student, and a firm refined mouth, a face expressive of soul and intellect, in which the fires of passion are quenched, and the angel of purity has set his mark.

History on Canvas.

A striking picture is "Charles I. leaving Westminister Hall, after his trial." He is passing through the street, followed by a guard; a fine looking man, but his face is deathly pale and careworn. As he passes a corner, a handsome, richly-dressed royalist looks upon him with the utmost pity, and bows with reverent air; while, on the other side, the rabble amongst which are blacksmiths with pincers in hand fresh from the forges, taunt and revile him as he passes.

The "Landing of the Puritans" is a fine Spanish picture, full of interest. The minister and his little flock are engaged in prayer. He holds the Bible, with hands upraised, while some of them are kneeling, some prostrate, and all devout. In the background are seen the sea and ship.

"The Eve of Battle" represents Joan of Arc, the peasant girl of France, dressed in military accoutrements, bearing the national standard, and leading a procession of priests, who are conducting a religious ceremony. As she passes, the bowmen, on each side, bow and kneel, and hail her as their victorious leader.

The "Landing of Columbus" is a fine Spanish painting, representing the great discoverer, wrinkled and careworn, with flowing white hair, holding in one hand the standard of Spain; the other, holding his sword on the neck of a prostrate savage. A priest bears the crucifix, and the savages look with wonder, and the men with reverent awe. The ship and sea are in the background.

An English picture, " The Night before Bosworth," represents Richard III. in his dream, the night before the battle of Bosworth. He is sleeping in his bed-chamber, his hands clutching the sheets, his face upturned, and his mouth open, as the terrible visions flit through his mind. On the floor lie his sword, armor and jewels.

" The fall of Rienzi, the last Roman Tribune," is a large English picture. Rienzi, finding the people clamorous for his death, is attempting to escape from the capitol, by throwing a robe over him; but a fierce soldier, with lowering brow, and dagger in hand, has snatched the robe from his head, and he is discovered. A toothless hag is shouting an alarm, for the populace to gather at the scene.

No language can depict the horrors of war, as is done by a picture, entitled " Cæsar," in a few square yards of canvas; no moralist can so illustrate the inherent wickedness of a selfish ambition. Cæsar is shown riding on a spirited charger, his face is fine and intellectual, but cold and stern,—his eye intently fixed on a globe, which he holds before him. On his brow is the conqueror's wreath, and he is preceded by two

shrouded figures, mowing all down before them. One of his
horses hoofs, is crushing the body of a beautiful female, who
lies prostrate on the the ground, powerless to rise. Before
his horses feet, and about to be trampled on, are several prostrate figures,—one a man with face full of energy, with head
upraised, and looking at the conqueror with the utmost hate
and fury; while another with clenched hands, and mouth open,
is expiring in agony. Before him an affrighted mother is
fleeing, her face white with terror. She holds her lovely, but
terrified infant, and grasps a broken column, to support her
sinking body. On the steps she is about to ascend, lies a
sickening pool of blood. The broken column lies on the
ground, a blighted tree is shaken by the blast of war, the
horrid night birds are abroad, while in the distance the hori-
zon is reddened by the devouring conflagration of falling cities.   Above flying through the air, is the goddess of war and
desolation, with flashing eyes, and open mouth, her black
hair and robes streaming behind her, holding a drawn sword
in her right hand extended forward, and in her left, behind
her, a torch of flames.   Behind, the sky is lurid with burning
cities and palaces.   To all this, the conqueror is heedless,—
his eye is fixed on the globe before him—his ears are stopped,
and his heart closed by the vaulting devil of ambition, which
has taken possession of his soul. This is the history of the
grim past, epitomized.

Pencilings of the Antique.

A striking picture is "Circe and the companions of Ulysses," in which Circe is represented as a fair, golden haired maiden, watching the herd of disgusting swine, into which she had changed the followers of Ulysses by her magic potions. She is arrayed in a white robe, and is seated on an elevation, which the angry swine attempt in vain to reach. Another picture based on mythological lore, is "Ulysses and the Sirens." The vessel of Ulysses is passing the island on which the Sirens dwelt; and to guard himself from their melodious voices, he had stopped the ears of his men with wax, and bound himself to the mast, and ordered his men to give no heed to his commands until they had passed the enchanting isle. The beautiful Sirens, with harp and timbrel beckon him to come, but the vessel keeps on her way unturned.

The "Chariot Race" recalls the mad excitement of the Roman races. The immense amphitheatre is crowded, and two swarthy bareheaded charioteers are madly urging their foaming steeds to their utmost speed. Each is driving four beasts, and the race is evenly balanced. The excitement of the horses, drivers and populace, is expressed in an astonishing manner.

One of the most wonderful works of art, is a table top in mosaic, from Florence, which has inlaid in it seventeen thousand different pieces of marble, and which required three men seven years to make. The design is music, musical instruments, scientific and other apparatus, flowers, etc., and every part, even to every note of music, is a separate piece of marble. This is priced at $10,000.

A remarkable picture is the "Death of Cæsar." He has fallen; the fatal stroke has been given, and his blood stains his robe, and the rich pavement. His eyes are already glazing, in death, but as Brutus comes up, he looks reproachfully at him. A citizen is hastening away covering his face, and another throwing up his hands in horror.

Famous Masters.

By famous masters, we do not mean old masters, but those whose works are here, and who have a worldwide fame. The most remarkable is " Christ," painted by Murillo, and is the scene of the crucifixion. Christ is hanging on the cross, thick darkness about him, the body white and ghastly in the gloom, the hair matted, the crown of thorns pressed down on the bleeding brow, the face in the shadow — altogether, a wonderfully vivid and impressive picture.

The "Crucifixion," by Vandyke, is also marvelous. The head leans, as if he were writhing in unutterable torture, the face is pallid from exhaustion, the eyes shrouded with shadows, and have a piteous, agonized, yet patient look, that thrills one to the heart: the mouth is open, as if gasping in agony; the blood streams from the nail wounds, and the expression of suffering is wonderful.

Landseer is represented by a picture of a lion, which shows that his fame is well earned, as one of the greatest painters of animals, of any period.

Turner, the great marine painter, is represented by a view of a castle in Wales; but it does not realize one's expectations, when the fame of the artist is considered.

Queen Victoria lent a large painting by Benjamin West, "The Death of Gen. Wolfe," which is a grand representation of that tragic event.

There is a portrait of Sir Joshua Reynolds, by himself, which does not impress most people as particularly fine, and several portraits by Sir Peter Lely, are not what would be considered good to-day. The picture of a peasant girl, by

Dubufe, and a sheep's head, by Rosa Bonheur, both on one canvass, are much admired.

Sermons on the Wall.

The picture from the Swedish gallery, "The Five Foolish Virgins at the locked Door," is a good text. The beautiful maidens are robed in rich attire, and bear lamps, which, except two, have gone out. One is kneeling before the locked door with uplifted arms, imploring an entrance; another is crouching to the earth in despair. One of dark and stately beauty stands erect, her face defiant, and flashing with indignation, while another with golden hair and faultless features, is pressing forward, as if there was yet hope. Another is already indifferent and has turned away. We can almost imagine their ringing cry,—

> No light! so late! and dark and chill the night;
> Oh, let us in, that we may find the light!
> Have we not heard the Bridegroom is so sweet?
> Oh, let us in, that we may kiss his feet!

And then the mournful response from within,

> Too late! Too late! Ye can not enter now.

Like a blast from a bugle, "Paul at Athens," rouses one's enthusiasm, at the thought of a sublime purpose, and consecrated life. His mantle is tattered, his bare feet travel-stained, his face furrowed by dark lines of care and suffering, his sunken eyes framed in black shadows, his hands and arms tanned and shrunken, until the corded muscles and blue arteries, stand out from the wasted flesh, and yet, he stands before the proud philosophers of Athens, and holds them awe-struck by the sublime revelation,—"Whom therefore ye ignorantly worship, Him, declare, I unto you." By the side of this noble life, how pitifully small seem our lives, and the little purposes we cherish, how contemptible.

"The Anatomist," is a picture, that at once fastens attention. A professor with a fine intellectual face, yet stern and cold, is sitting in his easy chair, with the complacency of a man who has had an eminently successful career. Before him lies the subject for dissection,—the corpse of a beautiful young woman, covered by a sheet, one end of which he has raised, exposing the silken hair, tangled, and matted with filth, and the delicate features, crowned with a beauty that death could not destroy. This beauty, triumphant in death, has touched a chord of his frozen nature, and his cold eyes are fixed on the beautiful face in profound abstraction, as if wondering—

" Who was her father? Who was her Mother?
" Had she a sister? Had she a brother?
" Or was there a dearer one still, and a nearer one
" Yet than all other."

And so this picture preaches a sermon on the frailties of human nature, and the need of Christian charity.

"Early Affliction" is a most exquisite picture of a peasant girl, traveling with bundle under her arm, who has left the village back in the distance, and is starting out among the pitfalls of the cruel world, to make her way as best she can. She has a face of angelic sweetness, her eyes show traces of tears, and she looks with open mouth and clasped hands, as if startled in the gathering darkness, and wondering what was before her. Not many can see it, without moistened eyes and softened heart, and the tender promise will be recalled: "When thy father and thy mother forsake thee, then the Lord will take thee up."

An expressive picture " My lady is a widow and childless," teaches us that "every heart hath its sorrows." A laborer returning home, is met in the field by his wife and baby, and has thrown down his spades, and caught up the crowing child. In the distance is a grand castle and park, and "my lady" dressed in black, and book in hand, is wandering listlessly down the gravelled walk, her beautiful face showing almost an envious expression, as she stands and watches the happy group, and is reminded of her own loneliness.

" The Family Scene, " a Russian picture, shows the divine mission of sorrow, to soften and purify the heart.

A mother and two daughters are in a luxurious sitting-room,—one at the piano, the other, a feeble invalid, sitting in an easy chair, languid and weak. You can almost hear the subdued tones of the piano, as the soft notes are touched to divert the sufferer,—and in the shadow sits the mother, looking at the invalid with an expression of unspeakable love, and parental solicitude.

"Lost and found" is an English picture of the prodigal son. From a vine covered cottage, in the midst of a charming English landscape, a white haired old man rushes out, followed by his daughter, to meet the returned prodigal, who is covered with rags, and has thrown himself on the ground in shame. The house-dog is bounding against him, and licking his face. The aged mother, with neat white cap, and a face worn, as if broken-hearted, is supported to the door, while the prim elder brother, looks out with coldness and unconcern.

"Young Whittington" is also an English picture, and is a lesson of hope to struggling young lives. The future Lord Mayor of London, is represented as a young lad, with fair open face, without a cap, with stick and bundle in hand, and traveling in the gathering darkness towards the spires of London, seen in the distance. He is stopping and listening with open ears and mouth to the great bell, and counting its strokes on his fingers.

A striking picture in the French gallery, is entitled "Herodias," and represents the beheading of John the Baptist. This martyrdom was one of those tragic events which art will ever sieze upon and perpetuate. Herodias the murderess, is reclining upon a couch of rich tapestry, but has partly raised herself up, to lift up the head of the Evangelist, which lies on a bloody napkin thrown across a platter, and has just been brought in by an Ethiopian slave. The artist has painted her truly—a fine Roman head with regular features and luxuriant black hair, but a cruel face, which even the sight of the glorious head of the martyred saint, with its kind, forgiving expression, and weird bloodless face, could not soften. Her black eyes are as cold, and her lips as pitiless, as before she did the accursed deed. She has the same stolid satisfaction, which the beast of prey feels, when watching his quivering victim, before it is devoured. Salome, perfect in form, and with the face of an angel, throws back the curtain at the door, as if afraid to enter, and is looking almost sadly and tenderly at the bloody sacrifice,—the fearful price of her folly and wickedness.

The "Prayer of Judith," is a striking picture, and represents the Jewish heroine, just preparing to strike the fatal blow at the tyrant of her oppressed race. Her magnificent figure, wrapped in a rich velvet robe, is thrown back, her large lustrous dark eyes upturned, and her rich strong, beautiful face, is lifted up, as if invoking the God of nations to give her strength to execute her daring purpose. In her left hand she holds a jewelled scimetar, her right upraised in invocation to heaven. The sleeping form of Holofernes is extended on a couch, covered with rich tapestry, entirely unmindful of his danger. The surroundings are suggestive of Oriental splendor,—the leopard skin on the floor, the elaborate ebony carving, the costly goblet and elegant tapestry, all suggest the royal rank of the tyrant. The picture teaches a lesson of heroic resolution, and of reliance on Divine help in times of emergency.

"Dark Moments," is a vivid representation of the struggles of genius. A handsome young artist is in his garret studio, from which he is about to be expelled. His face is buried in his hands in distress, and the motherly landlady looks at him with pity, yet is resolute in her design. A picture is on the easel, his palette and brushes are on the floor, the room is without a fire, and has a bare and proverty stricken appearance.

A most beautiful picture is "Christ Blessing Little Children," by Benjamin West. The Saviour is seated with a wondering child in his arms, while the happy mother kneels before him radiant with joy. Another little child is leaning lovingly against him, while a third is peering shyly over its shoulder.   Others are also bringing their children, while the grave disciples look reverently at the beautiful sight.

A Medley of Art Gems.

In the British gallery is a picture which is almost startling in its strangeness, and which arrests the eye at once, by its somber shadows and deep mysterious meaning. That unfathomable reverence for mystery, which is inseparable from our existence, and whose depths no plummet e'er has sounded, here finds food for its fancy; and we turn again and again to the strange conception of the artist, which awakens to new life the drooping powers of the imagination, and sends them forth to make fresh discoveries and conquests in the realm of the great unknown. The picture is called "Lenore," and is founded on a wild German legend, something like this: Lenore, a beautiful maiden, has a lover in the distant wars. After they are ended, the victorious legions come back, and march with waving banners and joyous measure through the glad streets of their nation's capital. Lenore watches the triumphal procession with anxious eyes to greet the return of her lover, but she watches and waits in vain. In her disappointment, she becomes heart-sick and melancholy; and she has a vision in which she imagines that her betrothed calls for her at the dead of night, mounted on his war horse, to convey her that very night to their nuptials, a hundred leagues away. He takes her before him on his steed, and as they swiftly plunge through the darkness, they pass through the most ghastly horrors. The artist has seized this wild legend, and made it the subject of one of the most weird pictures in the whole collection of paintings. It is a night scene; the ominous birds of darkness are flying abroad. A procession is led by a weeping angel, and followed by four repulsive hags, who are draped in shrouds, and bear flaming torches, which throw a sickly, ghastly light over the scene. Then follows the warrior on his gallant charger, his hair streaming in the wind, his eyes distended with horror, and bearing the maiden on his saddle before him. The steed is also affrighted,—from his panting nostrils issues the fierce blast of his hot breath,—his eyes are flashing with terror, for at his side a furious surf is dashing, as if to engulf them, and struggling in the frightful flood, are four beautiful females, one of whom, half prostrate,—her golden hair falling loosely beneath her, has seized the bridle, and is clinging to it with the clutch of despair. Another with her long black hair streaming behind her is throwing up her arms beseechingly toward the rider, while another with shroud over her head, is in an attitude of hopelessness. Behind the group are seen a procession of hooded spectres, while away

in the distance, discerned through the sickly light, the dim
outline of a gigantic figure is seen approaching, followed by
a company of shadowy human shapes just discernable in the
retreating darkness.   This strange conception is expressed on
the canvas with wonderful power, and gives to the picture a
weird fascination.

" Memory " is a statue in granite, of a female figure at the
time of life in which the blush of youthful loveliness merges
into the calm repose of mature beauty. She holds a wreath
of flowers which it may be supposed represents all the bright
hued freshness and fragrance of the present; but from this,
she has turned her eyes, and her thoughts ramble listlessly
back, down the dim vista of the past.

Vandyke was a fortunate artist, in living at the time of the
cavaliers, in a romantic and chivalrous age, when costumes
were rich and imposing in the extreme, and personal beauty
was the supreme test of popular favor. For instance, compare our modern costume in point of display, with that
which appears in this portrait by Vandyke, of Owen Abbott,
whose chief claim to immortality seems to consist in the fact
that he was deputed to conduct George the First to his throne.
The picture shows a full, handsome, cheery, fresh face, set in
a flowing wig, like a beautiful picture in a silver casing, a
graceful and well-proportioned figure set off by a red velvet
cloak, which gives as much life to the picture, as the same rich

MEMORY.

tints to a tulip. The attitude is fine, the mien courtly and dignified, and the portrait is probably one of the best efforts of the artist, and reveals to us something of the splendor of personal adornment in that period of English history.

At the Centennial anniversary of the battle of Concord, a statue was erected at Concord, Massachusetts, called "The Minute Man of 1775." Here is the model from which the bronze statue was cast, which is well worthy of careful study. There is a sense of strength and vigor about this, that almost inspires one with heroic purpose. There is a dash,— a determination about it, that makes one feel that the minute man was not a' machine for parade, but a hero from principle. It represents a young man, with fine face, but scowling, as if some unprovoked outrage had been committed, and none but he could settle the difficulty. His left hand rests on the plough, which he is just leaving like Cincinattus of old, while in his right, he grasps his old flint musket,—his powder horn slung behind him. He has thrown his coat across the plough out of the way, his collar is thrown back, and his sleeves are rolled up, showing the powerful muscles of his strong arms. His long hair is thrown back, and the side of his hat is turned up, and he seems the very impersonation of fearlessness, guided by a sublime purpose. It is the work of D. C. French, an American artist, and is deservedly a recognized acquisition to American art.

In the French department is a life size bronze statue which at once attracts notice. It is called " The Priestess of Isis," which was one of the principal Egyptian divinities. There is something so striking about this, that it carries the mind back without difficulty, thousands of years to the remote civilization of Egypt. The face is of the Egyptian type,— flat nose, thick lips, and a low forehead, but yet is pleasing and impressive. The upper part of the body is naked, except a head-dress, rich and showy, and heavy bracelets on arms and wrists. Around the waist is a loose skirt, beneath which are seen the sandals and anklets. Before her stands a harp, with frame of bright variegated colors, on which she is playing; but she leans forward and looks intently as if spell-bound by some revelation in the distance.

Here we see the "Death of Abel," in which the artist has pictured the scene of earth's first tragedy. The body of the murdered Abel lies on the ground,—a sickening pool of blood oozing from his head. Adam, full bearded and of strong vigorous frame, bends over it, with head bent down as if in shame and grief. His hands are clenched as if in agony, until the veins seem ready to burst. Beautiful Eve by his side leans one arm against him, as if for consolation and support, and with the other hides her face, and shuts the horrid spectacle from her eyes. Her head is bowed to the earth, as if ready to sink under the weight of her affliction, and her long golden hair falls to the ground as if to complete the picture of despair.

A picture in the United States gallery called "The Boston boys and General Gage," illustrates a favorite story with boys, and the subject is capitally handled. A delegation of boys have called at the quarters of General Gage to relate their grievances. He has come to the door to hear their story, and stands good-naturedly in his military suit of red coat and yellow vest and breeches, two of his aids looking curiously on, while a mischievous negro boy looks slyly out of the window, his face in a broad grin. The boys, dressed in gayly colored coats, have hats off, except one little fellow who is perfectly indifferent to the presence of rank, and stands holding his sled, entirely unconcerned. The spokesman of the party, a handsome boy, is relating their wrongs, with hat in hand and skates strapped on his side, while a venerable gentleman of the old school, stands back almost shocked by the proceeding, and wondering what it will come to. He feels some uneasiness about it—perhaps he has a grandson in the crowd, and he wants to see how it will end. A negro nurse with baby is gazing very intently, and picks up what information she can. At a short distance a little scamp is climbing the lamp-post, to the horror of the soldier on guard who hastens to drive him off; while another sentinel is turning his head back to see a very pretty young lady who is crossing the streets, and coquettishly holding up her skirts.

We next notice a picture called "The Vanquished," which is a scene in a Roman Palace. The majestic columns, costly marble pavement, bronze statues, and walls ornamented with designs of different colors, indicate an abode of luxurious elegance.

The vanquished gladiator stands leaning against a column, a man of magnificent physique, whose muscles are like thews of steel, but a face lowering with the rage and indignation of defeat. His black shaggy hair and beard, his lowering brow, his piercing black eyes that might belong to a beast of prey, his hand clutching his hair, as if he would tear it out by the roots, are all ablaze with the vexation of his turbulent spirit. His dog stands near, with head leaning against him as if he had a human sympathy. A beautiful woman with auburn hair and sweet, noble countenance, has clasped his arm, endeavoring to appease his anger and soothe his disappointment, but apparently has failed to calm the stormy nature of the man of violence.

We will next notice a picture in the Belgium gallery called "Dante and the Young Girls of Florence." The great poet is represented as sitting at the foot of a stairway; wearied and spent by continual thought, his head leans on the rail, and he has fallen asleep, with his book lying before him, and his arm across his breast, while three fair maidens with golden hair are lingering near him, as if doubtful whether to break his slumbers or to leave him undisturbed. The pure, blonde beauty of the maidens, in their rich attire of satin and figured silk, the red, flowing robe of the poet, the fine profile of his intellectual face, sad and musing in slumber, as if unable to forget the revelations of the "Inferno," all form a picture of great attractiveness to the intellectual observer.

But we turn to a strange picture, entitled "Sheikh Salah Dead in his Tent," which has a weird and ghastly appearance, and yet is invested with a strange fascination. The fallen chief is lying on the floor, on rich tapestry, and a lion's skin, the lower part of his body covered with a white robe,—his musket and pistols by his side, and his turban on his head. His features are of the strongest Arab type,—dark sunken eyes, thick lips, and a thin straggling black beard and mustache. A lamp at the feet of the corpse, casts a ghastly light over the scene, but discloses a group of mourners, probably his wives, who are sitting over the dead body, shrouded in white hoods, through which their faces are visible. One covers her face with both hands, as if to shut out the mournful sight; another, a young and beautiful face, gazes with an intensely sad expression from her large dark eyes, and sits with clasped hands as if uncontrollable in her grief; while an older woman, further back, looks on with apparent composure, and accepts the affliction with philo-sophical resignation.

A picture in the United States gallery, called "Christians in the Dungeon of the Coliseum, " is a reminder of the dark reign of blood and superstition which sought to crush the infant Christian church, and which brought to martyr-dom many glorious souls, of which the world was not worthy. The scene is in a dungeon, separated from the Coliseum by an iron wicket gate, in which are a group of Chris-tian captives awaiting their doom. In the foreground a maiden with long, sunny hair and beautiful face, stands with supplicating face upraised to heaven in prayer,—her left arm covering her naked breasts, and her right clasping the hand of her husband, or lover, who is seated by her, his head downcast, as if sinking under the burden of utter hope-lessness. A Roman soldier in armor of mail, and with hel-met and spear, has rudely grasped her, and is pointing to the terrible scene in the arena, thus reminding them of their fate. To the right a young man and woman are seated closely together with crucifix in hand, while near them sit an aged man and wife, with white hair and venerable aspect,—the aged mother supporting the head of her daugh-ter; while near a younger mother is fainting under the ter-rible trial, and falling unconsciously to the floor, where her beautiful infant is innocently playing.

Through the open door, the arena is seen, gallery above gallery, crowded with cruel spectators. In the arena a fierce Numidian lion of massive form, and shaggy mane, has sprung upon a Christian martyr, and buried his cruel claws in his flesh,—the blood streaming down, while the poor martyr in his agony, is supporting himself by clinging to the side of the arena. The blood-thirsty multitude are wild with excitement, and are bending forward, anxious to glut their eyes by a feast of blood.

In the United States gallery is a beautiful picture called " Canada Otter," by Audubon, the celebrated naturalist. A fine otter is descending on a log to a stream. His mouth is open, and he shows his teeth as if he were expecting an attack from some unknown quarter. The exquisite coloring and shading of the fur, the strikingly natural position of the animal, and the tints of the foliage filling the background, are as true to Nature as might be expected from an artist who held communion with her in her great solitudes for years.

A most suggestive picture is " The Pilgrim's Sunday Morning," in the U. S. gallery. A company of pilgrims are plodding through the snow on their way to the log church seen in the distance. The two stalwart leaders, dressed with peaked hats, wide white collars, belts and leggins, march with their trusty rifles in one hand, and their bibles in the other.

They are followed by the saintly looking old minister, and his sweet faced daughter, while following are young mothers with infants in arms, old women tottering with the weight of years, and the bright happy faces of children,—the little band being protected in the rear by the valiant fathers and husbands, who are thoroughly armed, ready for any emergency. The landscape has a most desolate, forbidding look, and it is apparently one of those clear cold mornings so common in the rigorous Northern winters. Would that every effeminate and unworthy descendant of such noble ancestery could see this expressive scene, and drink in the lesson of self-denial and devotion to duty which it suggests. It is a fit rebuke to our luxury loving age and people, when the noble discipline of self-sacrifice seems almost sometimes well nigh a remembrance of the past.

Some of the most remarkable works of art are pictures in mosaic in the Italian department. Here is a picture nearly six feet in width and about two feet high, which at a distance looks like an oil painting, so smooth and fresh seem the colors, but what is our astonishment when we look closely, to perceive that this elaborate scene with all its diversity of coloring and design is made up of differently colored pieces of stone, each scarcely larger than a pin head, and so wonderfully set together as to produce this pleasing effect. The scene is an Italian landscape and represents the ruins of the Temple of Pæstum, near Naples. The sky is blue and soft, and the outlines of the mountains in the distance are mellowed by the hazy atmosphere. In the foreground are the ruins of the massive temple, its roof nearly fallen to decay, but some of its majestic columns still standing, the stately monuments of its former glory; while fragments of others covered with rich carvings, are scattered around in indiscriminate confusion. Near it, is a pool whose placid surface reflects the hues of the rich sunlight, and a group of cattle are cooling themselves in its refreshing waters, while, not far distant are two shepherds in the picturesque costume of the country, attended by their faithful dog. On the right is an extended plain, across which a horseman is furiously galloping towards the beautiful city of Naples in the distance, the dim outline of whose lofty domes and imposing edifices bear witness to its elegance and grandeur.

When we consider that this elaborate picture is composed of these tiny stones joined together with such exquisite skill and infinite patience that it requires a close inspection to distinguish the joints between them, no wonder we are amazed at such a triumph not only of artistic taste, but also of tireless perseverance.

A magnificent picture, "Marriage of the Prince of Wales at Windsor, 1863," lent by Queen Victoria, is nearly always surrounded by an admiring throng. It is about six feet square, and although it represents the imposing edifice, as it was, filled with the most distinguished and noble of the realm, dressed in the most elaborate court costume, yet in that sea of faces and figures, every one is a portrait, finished with the utmost delicacy and perfection. It has an accuracy of detail, and such an exquisite softness and clearness of finish, as to make it a marvel of beauty.

A very interesting picture, "Washing the Beggars feet, on Maundy-Thursday," is a very striking representation of an ancient custom which required the nobility on that day to humble themselves by this menial service. The beggars are seated in a row, with feet bared, and they are a study truly. One has his head bound up with a white cloth, another has a bandage over the left eye, one, an old woman, red-faced, blear-eyed and wrinkled, sits with her hands clasped in peaceful submission, her face beaming with satisfaction at the humiliation of her betters, while another, an old man with a saintly face and long, venerable white locks, sits with folded hands and meek expression, while his feet are being washed by the noble lord who stoops over him, and whose handsome figure is covered with a rich figured velvet cloak trimmed with ermine. Behind the nobleman stands his wife, a beautiful lady with blue eyes and golden hair, dressed in rich furs, and also his son, a handsome boy clad in elegantly embroidered robes, both of whom are witnessing the ceremony with great interest.

Every German is brought to a halt at once, at seeing a very large and spirited picture representing the Crown Prince of Germany and his staff on the battle field. They are mounted and galloping abreast, the Prince a little in advance, and as we look, we can almost fancy that the noble steeds are bounding towards us, and that we can hear the clatter of their hoofs. The figures are wonderfully life-like, and the picture is one of the most spirited and animated in the collection.

In the British gallery is an admirable portrait of Lady Marianne Alford, lent by the Earl of Brownlow, which represents a lady of surpassing loveliness. We see a magnificent full length figure, life size,—a face so fair and fresh that it would seem to be the chosen home of health, happiness and purity; and when we notice the queenly poise of the head, the exquisitely moulded hands and arms, and the expression, combining native dignity and charming simplicity, we cannot but admire the rare taste and wondrous skill of the artist in thus transmitting to canvas, some of those subtle and delicate graces which are the crowning excellency of glorious womanhood, and which language is too gross and unwieldly to describe.

In the German gallery are two large paintings which illustrate that wonderful conception of genius—that immortal production of one of the world's great master minds,—Faust. The first is entitled "Marguerite" and represents the pure and confiding maiden bending in a transport of delight over the rich case of jewels which Faust has presented her. Guileless of evil, she is unaware that the costly gift, given to excite her vanity, is but the first step of that downward path which ends in her ruin. As she stands there, holding the gems before her in rapt admiration, her fair face radiant with wonder and grateful joy,—draped in her neat-fitting kirtle, her silken auburn hair confined by a simple cord,—she seems a perfect type of maidenly modesty, innocence and simplicity.

The other pictnre is "Marguerite in Prison," and represents her in a loathsome dungeon sitting on a bundle of straw, chained to the floor, but holding up the chain and looking at it with triumphant rapture, as if through the clanking of those cruel fetters, and the solitude of that dreary cell, she had found the sweet consolations of penitence. Near her stands Faust, his face buried in his hands, as if in unutterable anguish, while back in the gloom is the fiend Mephisto, dressed in flaming red, with horns protruding, holding a dim lantern, and looking on the scene before him with a horrible smile of exultation.

One might study for hours a picture in the British gallery called "Applicants for admission to a Casual Ward," which presents in the most eloquent manner the piteous destitution among the poor in London. It represents the exterior of a police station on a cold winter's morning, the ground covered

with snow and the air filled with frost. A large group are
waiting for admittance, amongst them an unfortunate trades-
man, who stands with clasped hands and bent form shivering
with the cold, and near him a respectable looking widow well
dressed with the remains of her once ample wardrobe, with
a child in her arms, and her little son standing beside her cry-
ing bitterly with the cold. Several inveterate topers and
vagrants with hardened and bloated faces, and rendered in-
sensible to the stinging cold by their vile potations, lean
against the wall in a half drunken stupor, and are dozing
away the weary moments; while near them stands a laboring
man with an honest, resolute face, as if determined to bear
up under his adversity, and holding his sleeping child,—his
wife weeping by his side as if completely discouraged, and
their three little children clinging to them for shelter and
protection. In the outskirts of the group are several gaunt,
ragged beggars who accept the situation as a matter of course,
and as a part of their common experience. No one can give
this a careful study, without having the sympathies of his
better nature aroused to genuine pity for the poor victims of
misfortune, who, alas, are too often forgotten in their times
of extremity. And so may this dumb, but yet eloquent canvas, become a powerful advocate to melt the hearts, and
move the sympathies of multitudes in the cause of sweet
charity.

But here is a picture so suggestive, that it commands our attention at once, and appeals with mute eloquence to the feelings of our better nature. It is called "The Tramp," and represents a middle-aged man in the glory of mature manhood, if computed by years, but in the shadows of old age, when measured by circumstances. Nature had endowed him with an honest face, which in better days must have been fine-looking, but which now is sadly marred by privations and despair. The eyes have become the firm seat of despondency; the face is no longer an index of thought and purpose, but it is abandoned to the fixed blank of hopelessness. His spirit has succumbed to the overwhelming tide of misfortune, and life has become a mechanical nonentity. He is covered by the ragged remains of a soldier's uniform; perhaps he has with undaunted heart, endured the tedious marches of perilous campaigns, and valiantly faced the foe on many a bloody field, but now his courage has vanished, and his resolution is no longer spurred by the memories of the past. Poor, homeless, hopeless wanderer, the type of weary thousands in our midst,—may the sun of a genial prosperity, and the sublime purposes of a resurrected manhood soon awake again to new melody, the long silent chords of thy sad, desponding heart.

And now dear reader, after visiting with me the numerous departments, and the many diversified objects of interest in this bewildering array of world treasures, with the hope that the remembrance of these grand sights may ever be a storehouse of happy and joyous memories, we will separate; but not until I shall have placed before you, as a fitting close, the more conspicuous and elaborate of the many literary tributes that graced the celebration of our Centennial Anniversary.

The National Ode.

BY BAYARD TAYLOR.

Recited by the author at the opening of our Centennial Exposition,
July 4, 1876.

I.—I.

Sun of the stately Day,
Let Asia into the shadow drift.
Let Europe bask in thy ripened ray,
And over the severing ocean lift
    A brow of broader splendor!
    Give light to the eager eyes
Of the land that waits to behold thee rise:
    The gladness of morning lend her,
    With the triumph of noon attend her,
    And the peace of the vesper skies!
    For lo! she cometh now
With hope on the lip and pride on the brow,
    Stronger, and dearer, and fairer,
    To smile on the love we bear her—
To live, as we dreamed her and sought her,
    Liberty's latest daughter!
In the clefts of the rocks, in the secret places,
    We found her traces;
On the hills, in the crash of woods that fall,
    We heard her call;
    When the lines of battle broke,
We saw her face in the fiery smoke;
Through toil, and anguish, and desolation,
    We followed and found her

With the grace of a virgin nation
    As a sacred zone around her!
        Who shall rejoice
        With a righteous voice,
Far-heard through the ages, if not she?
For the menace is dumb that defied her,
    The doubt is dead that denied her,
And she stands acknowledged, and strong, and free!

II.—I.

    Ah, hark! the solemn undertone
On every wind of human story blown.
    A large, divinely-molded Fate
Questions the right and purpose of a State,
        And in its plan sublime
        Our eras are the dust of Time.
        The far-off Yesterday of power
            Creeps back with stealthy feet,
    Invades the lordship of the hour,
And at our banquet takes the unbidden seat.
From all unchronicled and silent ages,
Before the Future first begot the Past,
        Till History dared, at last,
To write eternal words on granite pages;
From Egypt's tawny drift and Assur's mound,
    And where, uplifted white and fair,
    Earth highest yearns to meet a star,
And man his manhood by the Ganges found —
Imperial heads, of old millennial sway,
        And still by some pale splendor crowned,
Chill as a corpse-light in our full-orbed day,
        In ghostly grandeur rise
And say, through stony lips and vacant eyes:
"Thou that assertest freedom, power and fame,
        Declare to us thy claim!"

I.—II.

On the shores of a continent cast,
    She won the inviolate soil
By loss of heirdom of all the Past,
And faith in the royal right of Toil!
She planted homes on the savage sod:
    Into the wilderness lone
        She walked with fearless feet,
        In her hand the divining rod,
        Till the veins of the mountains beat
With fire of metal and force of stone!
        She set the speed of the river-head
        To turn the mills of her bread;
She drove her plowshare deep
Through the prairies' thousand-centuried sleep;
        To the South, and West, and North,
        She called the Pathfinder forth,
    Her faithful and sole companion,
Where the flushed Sierra, snowy-starred,
        Her way to the sunset barred,
And the nameless rivers in thunder and foam
    Channeled the terrible canyon!
    Nor paused till her uttermost home
Was built in the smile of a softer sky,
    And the glory of beauty still to be,
Where the haunted waves of Asia die
    On the strand of the world-wide sea!

II.—II.

The race, in conquering,
Some fierce Titanic joy of conquest knows;
    Whether in veins of serf or king
Our ancient blood beats restless in repose.
    Challenge of Nature unsubdued

Awaits not man's defiant answer long;
　　For hardship, even as wrong,
Provokes the level-eyed, heroic mood.
This for herself she did ; but that which lies,
　　As over earth the skies,
Blending all forms in one benignant glow,—
　　Crowned conscience, tender care,
Justice, that answers every bondman's prayer,
Freedom where Faith may lead or Thought may dare,
　　The power of minds that know,
　　Passion of hearts that feel,
　　Purchased by blood and woe,
　　Guarded by fire and steel—
Hath she secured ?　What blazon on her shield,
　　In the clear Century's light
　　Shines to the world revealed,
Declaring nobler triumph, born of Right ?

I.—III.

Foreseen in the vision of sages,
　　Foretold when martyrs bled,
She was born of the longing of ages,
　　By the truth of the noble dead
　　And the faith of the living fed!
No blood in her lightest veins
Frets at remembered chains,
Nor shame of bondage has bowed her head.
　　In her form and features still,
　　The unblenching Puritan will,
　　Cavalier honor, Huguenot grace,
　　The Quaker truth and sweetness,
And the strength of the danger-girdled race
Of Holland, blend in a proud completeness.
From the homes of all, where her being began,
　　She took what she gave to man :

Justice, that knew no station,
        Belief, as soul decreed,
    Free air for aspiration,
Free force for independent deed!
    She takes, but to give again,
As the sea returns the rivers in rain;
And gathers the chosen of her seed
From the hunted of every crown and creed.
Her Germany dwells by a gentler Rhine;
Her Ireland sees the old sunburst shine;
Her France pursues some dream divine;
Her Norway keeps his mountain pine;
Her Italy waits by the western brine;
    And, broad-based under all,
Is planted England's oaken-hearted wood,
    As rich in fortitude
As e'er went worldward from the island-wall!
    Fused in her candid light,
To one strong race all races here unite:
Tongues melt in hers, hereditary foemen
Forget their sword and slogan, kith and clan;
    'Twas glory, once, to be a Roman;
She makes it glory, now, to be a man!

II.—III.

        Bow down!
    Doff thine æonian crown!
        One hour forget
    The glory, and recall the debt;
        Make expiation,
        Of humbler mood,
    For the pride of thine exultation
O'er peril conquered and strife subdued!
    But half the right is wrested
        When victory yields her prize,

And half the marrow tested
          When old endurance dies. *
In the sight of them that love thee,
Bow to the Creater above thee!
          He faileth not to smite
          The idle ownership of Right,
Nor spares to sinews fresh from trial,
          And virtue schooled in long denial,
The tests that wait for thee
In larger perils of prosperity.
          Here, at the Century's awful shrine,
          Bow to thy Fathers' God, and thine!

I.—IV.

          Behold!   She bendeth now,
Humbling the chaplet of her hundred years;
There is a solemn sweetness on her brow,
          And in her eyes are sacred tears.
          Can she forget,
In present joy, the burden of her debt,
          When for a captive race
          She grandly staked and won
The total promise of her power begun,
          And bared her bosom's grace
To the sharp wound that inly tortures yet?
          Can she forget
          The million graves her young devotion set,
          The hands that clasp above,
From either side, in sad, returning love?
          Can she forget,
Here, where the ruler of today,
          The citizen of tomorrow
And equal thousands to rejoice and pray,
          Beside these holy walls are met—
Her birth-cry, mixed of keenest bliss and sorrow?

Where, on July's immortal morn,
  Held forth, the people saw her head
And shouted to the world, "The King is dead,
    But lo! the Heir is born!"
When fire of youth, and sober trust of age,
In farmer, soldier, priest and sage,
    Arose and cast upon her
Baptismal garments — never robes so fair
  Clad prince in old-world air —
Their lives, their fortunes, and their sacred honor!

II.—IV.

  Arise! Recrown thy head,
Radiant with blessings of the dead!
  Bear from this hallowed place
The prayer that purifies thy lips,
The light of courage that defies eclipse,
The rose of man's new morning on thy face!
  Let no iconoclast
Invade thy rising pantheon of the past,
  To make a blank where Adams stood,
To touch the Father's sheathed and sacred blade,
Spoil crowns on Jefferson and Franklin laid,
Or wash from Freedom's feet the stain of Lincoln's blood!
  Hearken, as from that haunted hall
  Their voices call:
    "We lived and died for thee;
We greatly dared that thou might'st be;
    So, from thy children still
We claim denials which at last fulfill,
And freedom yielded to preserve the free!
  Beside clear-hearted Right,
That smiles at Power's uplifted rod,
  Plant Duties that requite
And Order that sustains, upon thy sod,

And stand in stainless might
Above all self, and only less than God!"

III.—I.

Here may thy solemn challenge end,
All-proving Past, and each discordance die
Of doubtful augury;
Or in one choral with the Present blend,
And that half-heard, sweet harmony
Of something nobler that our sons may see!
Though poignant memories burn
Of days that were, and may again return,
When thy fleet foot, O Huntress of the Woods,
The slippery brinks of danger knew,
And dim the eyesight grew
That was so sure in thine old solitudes—
Yet stays some richer sense,
Won from the mixture of thine elements,
To guide the vagrant scheme,
And winnow truth from each conflicting dream!
Yet in thy blood shall live
Some force unspent, some essence primitive,
To seize the highest use of things:
For Fate, to mold thee to her plan,
Denied thee food of kings,
Withheld the udder and the orchard fruits,
Fed thee with savage roots,
And forced thy harsher milk from barren breasts of man!

III.—II.

O sacred Woman-form!
Of the first people's need and passion wrought,
No thin, pale ghost of thought,
But fair as morning, and as heart's blood warm—
Wearing thy priestly tiar on Judah's hills;

Clear-eyed beneath Athené's helm of gold;
　　　Or from Rome's central seat
Hearing the pulses of the continents beat
　　　In thunder where her legions rolled,
Compact of high, heroic hearts and wills,
　　　Whose being circles all
The selfish aims of men, and all fulfills;
Thyself not free, so long as one is thrall;
　　　Goddess, that as a nation lives,
　　　　　And as a nation dies,
That for her children as a man defies,
And to her children as a mother giyes —
　　　　Take our fresh fealty now!
No more a chieftainess, with wampum-zone
　　　　And feather-cinctured brow —
No more a new Britannia grown
To spread an equal banner to the breeze,
And lift thy trident o'er the double seas;
　　　　But with unborrowed crest,
In thine own native beauty dressed —
The front of pure command, the unflinching eye, thine own!

III.—III.

　　Look up, look forth, and on!
　　There's light in the dawning sky:
The clouds are parting, the night is gone;
　　Prepare for the work of the day!
　　Fallow thy pastures lie
　　And far thy shepherds stray,
And the fields of thy vast domain
　　Are waiting for purer seed
　　Of knowledge, desire, and deed,
For keener sunshine and mellower rain!
　　But keep thy garments pure:
Pluck them back, with the old disdain,

From touch of the hands that stain! '
So shall thy strength endure.
Transmute into good the gold of Gain,
Compel to beauty thy ruder powers,
   Till the bounty of coming hours
   Shall plant on thy fields apart,
With the oak of Toil, the rose of Art!
   Be watchful, and keep us so:
   Be strong, and fear no foe:
   Be just, and the world shall know!
With the same love love us, as we give;
   And the day shall never come,
   That finds us weak·or dumb
   To join and smite and cry
In the great task, for thee to die,
And the greater task, for thee to live!

THE CENTENNIAL ORATION.

Delivered by Hon. Wm. M. Evarts, at Philadelphia, July 4, 1876.

The event which to-day we commemorate supplies its own reflections and enthusiasms and brings its own plaudits. They do not at all hang on the voice of the speaker, nor do they greatly depend upon the contacts and associations of the place. The Declaration of American independence was, when it occurred, a capital transaction in human affairs; as such it has kept its place in history; as such it will maintain itself while human interest in human institutions shall endure. The scene and the actors, for their profound impression upon the world, at the time and ever since, have owed nothing to dramatic effects, nothing to epical exaggerations. To the eye there was nothing wonderful, or vast, or splendid, or pathetic in the movement or the display. Imagination or art can give no sensible grace or decoration to the persons, the place, or the performance, which made up the business of that day. The worth and force that belong to the agents and the action rest wholly on the wisdom, the courage and the faith that formed and executed the great design, and the potency and permanence of its operation upon the affairs of the world which, as foreseen and legitimate consequences, followed. The dignity of the act is the deliberate, circumspect, open and serene performance by these men in the clear light of day, and by a concurrent purpose, of a civic duty which embraced the greatest hazards to themselves and to all the people from whom they held this deputed discretion, but which, to their sober judgments, promised benefits to that people and their posterity, from generation to generation, exceeding these hazards and commensurate with its own fitness. The question of their conduct is to be measured by the actual weight and pressure of the manifold considerations which surrounded the subject before them, and by the abundant evidence that they comprehended their vastness and variety. By a voluntary and responsible choice they willed to do what was done, and what without their will would not have been done.

Thus estimated, the illustrious act covers all who participated in it with its own renown, and makes them forever conspicuous among men, as it is forever famous among events.   And thus the signers of the Declaration of our Independence "wrote their names where all nations should behold them, and all time should not efface them."   It was, "in the course of human events," intrusted to them to determine whether the fulness of time had come when a nation should be born in a day.   They declared the independence of a new nation in the sense in which men declare emancipation or declare war; the declaration created what was declared.

Famous, always, among men, are the founders of states, and fortunate above all others in such fame are these, our fathers, whose combined wisdom and courage began the great structure of our national existence, and laid sure the foundations of liberty and justice on which it rests.   Fortunate, first, in the clearness of their title and in the world's acceptance of their rightful claim.   Fortunate, next, in the enduring magnitude of the state they founded and the beneficence of its protection of the vast interests of human life and happiness which have here had their home.   Fortunate, again, in the admiring imitation of their work, which the institutions of the most powerful and most advanced nations more and more exhibit; and last of all, fortunate in the full demonstrations of our later time that their work is adequate to withstand the most disastrous storms of human fortunes, and survive unwrecked, unshaken and unharmed.

This day has now been celebrated by a great people at each recurrence of its anniversary for a hundred years, with every form of ostentatious joy, with every demonstration of respect and gratitude for the ancestral virtue which gave it its glory, and with the firmest faith that growing time should neither obscure its lustre nor reduce the ardor or discredit the sincerity of its observance.   A reverent spirit has explored the lives of the men who took part in the great transaction — has unfolded their characters and exhibited to an admiring posterity the purity of their motives, the sagacity, the bravery, the fortitude, the perseverance which marked their conduct, and which secured the prosperity and permanence of their work.

Philosophy has divined the secrets of all this power, and eloquence emblazoned the magnificence of all its results.   The heroic war which fought out the acquiescence of the Old World in the independence of the New; the

manifold and masterly forms of noble character and of patient and serene
wisdom which the great influences of the time begat; the large and splendid
scale on which these elevated purposes were wrought out, and the majestic
proportions to which they have been filled up; the unended line of eventful
progress, casting ever backward a flood of light upon the sources of the
original energy, and ever forward a promise and prophecy of unexhausted
power—all these have been made familiar to our people by the genius and
the devotion of historians and orators. The greatest statesmen of the Old
World for this same period of a hundred years have traced the initial steps in
these events, looked into the nature of the institutions thus founded ; weighed
by the Old-World wisdom, and measured by recorded experience, the probable fortunes of this new adventure on an unknown sea. This circumspect
and searching survey of our wide field of political and social experiments, no
doubt, has brought them a diversity of judgment as to the past, and of
expectation as to the future. But of the magnitude and the novelty and the
power of the forces set at work by the event we commemorate, no competent
authorities have ever greatly differed. The cotemporary judgment of Burke
is scarcely an overstatement of the European opinion of the immense import
of American independence. He declared: "A great revolution has hap-
pened—a revolution made, not by chopping and changing of power in any of
the existing states, but by the appearance of a new state, of a new species, in
a new part of the globe. It has made as great a change in all the relations
and balances and gravitations of power as the appearance of a new planet
would in the system of the solar world."

It is easy to understand that the rupture between the colonies and the
mother country might have worked a result of political independence that
would have involved no such mighty consequences as are here so strongly
announced by the most philosophic statesman of his age. The resistance of
the colonies, which came to a head in the revolt, was led in the name and for
the maintenance of the liberties of Englishmen against Parliamentary usur-
pation and a subversion of the British constitution. A triumph of those
liberties might have ended in an emancipation from the rule of the English
Parliament, and a continued submission to the scheme and system of the
British monarchy, with an American Parliament adjusted thereto, upon the
true principles of the English constitution. Whether this new political

establishment should have maintained loyalty to the British sovereign, or should have been organized under a crown and throne of its own, the transaction would then have had no other importance than such as belongs to a dismemberment of existing empire, but with preservation of existing institutions. There would have been, to be sure, a "new state," but not "of a new species;" and that it was "in a new part of the globe" would have gone far to make the dismemberment but a temporary and circumstantial disturbance in the old order of things. Indeed, the solidity and perpetuity of that order might have been greatly confirmed by this propagation of the model of the European monarchies on the boundless regions of this continent. It is precisely here that the Declaration of Independence has its immense importance. As a civil act, and by the people's decree — and not by the achievement of the army, or through military motives — at the first stage of the conflict it assigned a new nationality, with its own institutions, as the civilly, preordained end to be fought for and secured. It did not leave it to be an afterfruit of triumphant war, shaped and measured by military power, and conferred by the army on the people. This assured at the outset the supremacy of civil over military authority, the subordination of the army to the unarmed people. This deliberative choice of the scope and goal of the Revolution made sure of two things, which must have been always greatly in doubt, if military reasons and events had held the mastery over the civil power. The first was that nothing less than the independence of the nation and its separation from the system of Europe would be attained if our arms were prosperous; and the second, that the new nation would always be the mistress of its own institutions. This might not have been its fate had a triumphant army won the prize of independence, not as a task set for it by the people, and done in its service, but by its own might, and held by its own title, and so to be shaped and dealt with by its own will.

There is the best reason to think that the Congress which declared our independence gave its chief solicitude, not to the hazards of military failure, not to the chance of miscarriage in the project of separation from England; but to the grave responsibility of the military success (of which they made no doubt) and as to what should replace, as government to the new nation, the monarchy of England, which they considered as gone to them forever from the date of the Declaration.

Nor did this Congress feel any uncertainty, either in disposition or expectation, that the natural and necessary result would preclude the formation of the new government out of any other materials than such as were to be found in society as established on this side of the Atlantic. These materials, they foresaw, were capable of and would tolerate only such political establishment as would maintain and perpetuate the equality and liberty always enjoyed in the several colonial communities.

But all these limitations upon what was possible still left a large range of anxiety as to what was probable, and might become actual. One thing was too essential to be left uncertain, and the founders of this nation determined that there never should be a moment when the several communities of the different colonies should lose the character of component parts of one nation. By their plantation and growth up to the day of the Declaration of Independence they were subjects of one sovereignty, bound together in one political connection, parts of one country, under one constitution, with one destiny. Accordingly the Declaration, by its very terms, made the act of separation a dissolving by "one people" of "the political bands that have connected them with another," and the proclamation of the right and of the fact of independent nationality was "that these UNITED colonies are, and of right ought to be, free and independent States."

It was thus that, at one breath, "independence and union" were declared and established. The confirmation of the first by war, and of the second by civil wisdom, was but the execution of the single design, which it is the glory of this great instrument of our national existence to have framed and announced. The recognition of our independence first by France, and then by Great Britain, the closer union by the articles of confederation, and the final unity by the Federal Constitution, were all but muniments of title of that "liberty and union, one and inseparable," which were proclaimed at this place, and on this day, one hundred years ago, which have been our possession from that moment hitherto, and which we surely avow shall be our possession forever.

Seven years of revolutionary war and twelve years of consummate civil prudence brought us, in turn, to the conclusive peace of 1783 and to the perfected constitution of 1787. Few chapters of the world's history covering such brief periods are crowded with so many illustrious names, or made up of events of so deep and permanent interest to mankind. I cannot stay to recall to your attention these characters or these incidents, or to renew the gratitude and applause with which we never cease to contemplate them. It is only their relation to the Declaration of Independence itself that I need to insist upon, and to the new state which it brought into existence. In this view, these progressive processes were but the articulation of the members of the state, and the adjustment of its circulation to the new centres of its vital power. The processes were all implied and included in this political creation, and were as necessary and as certain, if it were not to languish and to die, as in any natural creature.

Within the .hundred years whose flight in our national history we mark to-day we have had occasion to corroborate by war both the independence and the unity of the nation. In our war against England for neutrality we asserted and we established the absolute right to be free of European entanglements, in time of war as well as in time of peace,'and so completed our independence of Europe. And by the war of the Constitution, a war within the nation, the bonds of our unity were tried and tested, as in a fiery furnace, and proved to be dependent on no shifting vicissitudes of acquiescence, no partial dissents or discontents; but, so far as is predicable of human fortunes, irrevocable, indestructible, perpetual! *Casibus hæc nullis, nullo delebilis ævo.*

We may be quite sure that the high resolve to stake the future of a great people upon a system of society and of polity that should dispense with the dogmas, the experience, the traditions, the habits and the sentiments upon which the firm and durable fabric of the British constitution had been built up was not taken without a solicitous and competent survey of the history, the condition, the temper, and the moral and intellectual traits of the people for whom the decisive step was taken.

It may indeed be suggested that the main body of the elements, and a large share of the arrangements, of the new government, were expected to be upon the model of the British system, and that the substantials of civil and religious liberty and the institutions for their maintenance and defense were already the possession of the people of England and the birthright of the colonists. But this consideration does not much disparage the responsibility assumed in discarding the correlative parts of the British constitution.

I mean the established church and throne; the permanent power of a hereditary peerage; the confinement of popular representation to the wealthy and educated classes; and the ideas of all participation by the people in their own government coming by gracious concession from the royal prerogative, and not by inherent right in themselves. Indeed, the counter consideration, so far as the question was to be solved by experience, would be a ready one. The foundation, and the walls, and the roof of this firm and noble edifice, it would be said, are all fitly framed together in the substantial institutions you propose to omit from your plan and model. The convenience and safety and freedom, the pride and happiness which the inmates of this temple and fortress enjoy, as the rights and liberties of Englishmen, are only kept in place and play because of the firm structure of these ancient strongholds of religion and law, which you now desert and refuse to build anew.

Our fathers had formed their opinions upon wiser and deeper views of man and Providence than these, and they had the courage of their opinions.

Tracing the progress of mankind in the ascending path of civilization, enlightenment and moral and intellectual culture, they found that the Divine ordinance of government, in every stage of the ascent, was adjustable on principles of common reason to the actual condition of a people; and always had for its objects, in the benevolent counsels of the Divine wisdom, the happiness, the expansion, the security, the elevation of society, and the redemption of man. They sought in vain for any title of authority of man over man, except of superior capacity and higher morality. They found the origin of castes and ranks, and principalities and powers, temporal or spiritual, in this conception. They recognized the people as the structure, the temple, the fortress, which the great Artificer all the while cared for and built up. As through the long march of time this work advanced, the forms and fashions of government seemed to them to be but the scaffolding and apparatus by which the development of a people's greatness was shaped and sustained. Satisfied that the people whose institutions were now to be projected had reached all that measure of strength and fitness of preparation for self-government which old institutions could give, they fearlessly seized the happy opportunity to clothe the people with the majestic attributes of their own sovereignty, and consecrate them to the administration of their own priesthood.

The repudiation by England of the spiritual power of Rome at the time of the Reformation was by every estimate a stupendous innovation in the rooted allegiance of the people, a profound disturbance of all adjustments of authority. But Henry VIII., when he displaced the dominion of the pope, proclaimed himself the head of the church. The overthrow of the ancient monarchy of France, by the fierce triumph of an enraged people, was a catastrophe that shook the arrangements of society from centre to circumference. But Napoleon, when he pushed aside the royal line of St. Louis, announced, "I am the people crowned," and set up a plebeian emperor as the impersonation and depositary, in him and his line forever, of the people's sovereignty. The founders of our commonwealth conceived that the people of these colonies needed no interception of the supreme control of their own affairs, no conciliations of mere names and images of power from which the pith and vigor of authority had departed. They, therefore, did not hesitate to throw down the partitions of power and right, and break up the distributive shares in authority of ranks and orders of men which, indeed, had ruled and advanced the development of society in civil and religious liberty, but might well be neglected when the protected growth was assured, and all tutelary supervision, for this reason, henceforth could only be obstructive and incongruous.

A glance at the fate of the English essay at a commonwealth, which preceded, and to the French experiment at a republic, which followed our own institution "of a new state, of a new species," will show the marvelous wisdom of our ancestors, which struck the line between too little and too much; which walked by faith indeed for things invisible, but yet by sight for things visible; which dared to appropriate everything to the people which belonged to Cæsar, but to assume for mortals nothing that belonged to God.

No doubt it was a deliberation of prodigious difficulty, and a decision of infinite moment, which should settle the new institutions of England after the execution of the king, and determine whether they should be popular or monarchical. The problem was too vast for Cromwell and the great men who stood about him, and, halting between the only possible opinions, they simply robbed the throne of stability, without giving the people the choice of their rulers. Had Cromwell assumed the state and style of king, and assigned the constitutional limits of prerogative, the statesmen of England would have anticipated the establishment of 1688, and saved the disgraces of the intervening record. If, on the other hand, the ever recurring consent of the people in vesting the chief magistracy had been accepted for the constitution of the state, the revolution would have been intelligible, and might have proved permanent. But what a "Lord Protector" was, nobody knew; and what he might grow to be, everybody wondered and feared. The aristocracy could endure no dignity above them less than a king's. The people knew the measure and the title of the chartered liberties which had been wrested or yielded from the king's prerogative; but what the division between them and a lord protector would be, no one could foreeast. A brief fluttering between the firmament above and the firm earth beneath, with no poise with either, and the discordant scheme was rolled away as a scroll. A hundred years afterward Montesquieu derided "this impotent effort of the English to establish a democracy," and divined the true cause of its failure. The supreme place, no longer sacred by the divinity that doth hedge about a king, irritated the ambitious, to which it was inaccessible except by faction and violence. "The government was incessantly changed, and the astonished people sought for democracy and found it nowhere. After much violence and many shocks and blows, they were fain to fall back upon the same government they had overthrown."

The English experiment to make a commonwealth without sinking its foundations into the firm bed of popular sovereignty necessarily failed. Its example and its lesson, unquestionably, were of the greatest service in sobering the spirit of English reform in government, to the solid establishment of constitutional monarchy, on the expulsion of the Stuarts, and in giving courage to the statesmen of the American Revolution to push on to the solid establishment of republican government, with the consent of the people as its everyday working force.

But if the English experiment stumbled in its logic by not going far enough, the French philosophers came to greater disaster by overpassing the lines which mark the limits of human authority and human liberty, when they undertook to redress the disordered balance between people and rulers, and renovate the government of France. To the wrath of the people against kings and priests they gave free course, not only to the overthrow of the establishment of the church and state, but to the destruction of religion and society. They deified man, and thought to raise a tower of man's building, as of old on the plain of Shinar, which should overtop the battlements of heaven, and frame a constitution of human affairs that should displace the providence of God. A confusion of tongues put an end to this ambition. And now out of all its evils have come the salutary checks and discipline in freedom, which have brought passionate and fervid France to the scheme and frame of a sober and firm republic like our own, and, we may hope, as durable.

How much, then, hung upon the decision of the great day we celebrate, and upon the wisdom and the will of the men who fixed the immediate, and if so the present, fortunes of this people. If the body, the spirit, the texture of our political life had not been collectively declared on this day, who can be bold enough to say when and how independence, liberty, union would have been combined, confirmed, assured to this people? Behold, now, the greatness of our debt to this ancestry, and the fountain, as from a rock smitten in the wilderness, from which the stream of this nation's growth and power takes its source. For it is not alone in the memory of their wisdom and virtues that the founders of a State transmit and perpetuate their influences in its lasting fortunes, and shape the character and purposes of its future rulers. "In the birth of societies," says Montesquieu, "it is the chiefs of a state that make its institutions; and afterward it is these institutions that form the chiefs of the state."

And what was this people, and what their traits and training, that could justify this congress of their great men in promulgating the profound views of government and human nature which the Declaration embodies, and expecting their acceptance as "self-evident"? How had their lives been disciplined, and how their spirits prepared, that the new-launched ship, freighted with all their fortunes, could be trusted to their guidance, with no chart or compass than these abstract truths? What warrant was there for the confidence that upon these plain precepts of equality of right, community of interest, reciprocity of duty, a polity could be framed which might safely discard Egyptian mystery, and Hebrew reverence, and Grecian subtlety, and Roman strength — dispense, even, with English traditions of

> "Primogenitive and due of birth,
> Prerogative of age, crown, sceptres, laurels"?

To these questions the answer was ready and sufficient. The delegates to this immortal assembly, speaking for the whole country, and for the respective colonies, their constituents, might well say:

"What we are, such are this people. We are not here as volunteers, but as their representatives. We have been designated by no previous official station, taken from no one employment or condition of life, chosen from the people at large because they cannot assemble in person, and selected because they know our sentiments, and we theirs, on the momentous question which our deliberations are to decide. They know that the result of all hangs on the intelligence, the courage, the constancy, the spirit of the people them-selves. If these have risen to a height and grown to a strength and una-nimity that our judgment measures as adequate to the struggle for independ-ence and the whole sum of their liberties, they will accept that issue and follow that lead. They have taken up arms to maintain their rights, and will not lay them down till those rights are assured. What the nature and sanc tions of this security are to be they understand must be determined by united counsels and concerted action. These they have deputed us to settle and proclaim, and this we have done to-day. What we have declared, the people will avow and confirm. Henceforth it is to this people a war for the defense of their united independence against its overthrow by foreign arms. Of that war there can be but one issue.

"And for the rest, as to the constitution of the new state, its species is disclosed by its existence. The condition of the people is equal, they have the habits of freemen, and possess the institutions of liberty. When the political connection with the parent state is dissolved, they will be self-governing and self-governed of necessity. As all governments in this world, good and bad, liberal or despotic, are of men, by men, and for men, this new state, having no caste or ranks, or degrees discriminating among men in its population, becomes at once a government of the people, by the people, and for the people. So it must remain, unless foreign conquest or domestic usur-pation shall change it. Whether it shall be a just, wise or prosperous gov-ernment, it must be a popular government, and correspond with the wisdom, justice and fortunes of the people."

And so this people, of various roots and kindred of the Old World—settled and transfused in their cisatlantic home into harmonious fellowship in

the sentiments, the interests, the habits, the affections which develop and
sustain a love of country — were committed to the common fortunes which
should attend an absolute trust in the primary relations between man and
his fellows and between man and his Maker. This Northern Continent of
America had been opened and prepared for the transplantation of the full-
grown manhood of the highest civilization of the Old World to a place where
it could be free from mixture or collision with competing or hostile elements,
and separated from the weakness and the burdens which it would leave
behind. The impulses and attractions which moved the emigration, and
directed it hither, various in form, yet had so much a common character as to
merit the description of being public, elevated, moral or religious. They
included the desire of new and better opportunities for institutions consonant
with the dignity of human nature, and with the immortal and infinite relations of the race. In the language of the times, the search for civil and
religious liberty animated the Pilgrims, the Puritans and the Churchmen, the
Presbyterians, the Catholics and the Quakers, the Huguenots, the Dutch and
the Walloons, the Waldenses, the Germans and the Swedes, in their several
migrations which made up the colonial population. Their experience and
fortunes here had done nothing to reduce, everything to confirm, the views and
traits which brought them hither. To sever all political relations, then, with
Europe, seemed to these people but the realization of the purposes which
had led them across the ocean — but the one thing needful to complete this
continent for their home, and to give the absolute assurance of that higher
life which they wished to lead. The preparation of the past and the enthusiasms of the future conspired to favor the project of self-government and
invest it with a moral grandeur which furnished the best omens and the best
guarantees for its prosperity. Instead of a capricious and giddy exaltation
of spirit, as at new-gained liberty, a sober and solemn sense of the larger
trust and duty took possession of their souls; as if the Great Master had
found them faithful over a few things, and had now made them rulers over
many.

These feelings, common to the whole population, were not of sudden
origin and were not romantic, nor had they any tendency to evaporate in
noisy boasts or run wild in air-drawn projects. The difference between
equality and privilege, between civil rights and capricious favors, between

freedom of conscience and persecution for conscience' sake, were not matters of moot debate or abstract conviction with our countıymen. The story of these battles of our race was the warm and living memory of their forefathers' share in them, for which, "to avoid insufferable grievances at home, they had been enforced by heaps to leave their native countries." They proposed to settle forever the question whether such grievances should possibly befall them or their posterity. They knew no plan so simple, so comprehensive, or so sure to this end as to solve all the minor difficulties in the government of society by a radical basis for its source, a common field for its operation, and an authentic and deliberate method for consulting and enforcing the will of the people as the sole authority of the state.

By this wisdom they at least would shift, within the sphere of government, the continuous warfare of human nature, on the field of good and evil, right and wrong,

> "Between whose endless jar justice resides,"

from conflicts of the strength of the many against the craft of the few. They would gain the advantage of supplying as the reason of the state the reason of the people, and decide by the moral and intellectual influences of instruction and persuasion the issue of who should make and who administer the laws. This involved no pretensions of the perfection of human nature, nor did it assume that at other times, or under other circumstances, they would themselves have been capable of self-government, or that other people then were or ever would be so capable. Their knowledge of mankind showed them that there would be faults and crimes so long as there were men. Their faith taught them that this corruptible would put on incorruption only when this mortal should put on immortality. Nevertheless, they believed in man and trusted in God, and on these imperishable supports they thought they might rest civil government for a people who had these living conceptions wrought into their own characters and lives.

The past and the present are the only means by which man foresees or shapes the future. Upon the evidence of the past, the contemplation of the present of this people, our statesmen were willing to commence a system which must continually draw, for its sustenance and growth, upon the virtue and vigor of the people. From this virtue and this vigor it can alone be nourished; it must decline in their decline, and rot in their decay. They traced this vigor and virtue to inexhaustible springs.   And, as the unspent heat of a lava soil, quickened by the returning summers, through the vintages of a thousand years,will still glow in the grape and sparkle in the wine, so will the exuberant forces of a race supply an unstinted vigor to mark the virtues of immense populations, and to the remotest generations.

To the frivolous philosophy of human life which makes all the world a puppet show, and history a book of anecdotes, the moral warfare which fills up the life of man and the record of his race seems as unreal and as aimless as the conflicts of the glittering hosts upon the airy field, whose display lights up the fleeting splendors of a northern night.   But free government for a great people never comes from or gets aid from such philosophers.   To a true spiritual discernment there are few things more real, few things more substantial, few things more likely to endure in this world than human thoughts, human passions, human interests, thus molten into the frame and model of our state.   *"O morem præclaram, disciplinamque, quam a major ibus accepimus, si quidem teneremus!"*

I have made no account, as unsuitable to the occasion, of the distribution of the national power between the General and the State governments, or of the special arrangements of executive authority, of the legislatures, courts and magistracies, whether of the General or of the State establishments. Collectively, they form the body and the frame of a complete government for a great, opulent and powerful people, occupying vast regions and embracing in their possessions a wide range of diversity of climate, of soil, and of all the circumstantial influences of external nature.   I have pointed your attention to the principle and the spirit of the government for which all this frame and body exist, to which they are subservient, and to whose mastery they must conform.   The life of the natural body is the blood, and the circulation of the moral and intellectual forces and impulses of the body politic shapes and molds the national life.   I have touched, therefore, upon the traits that determined this national life, as to be of, from and for the people, and not of, from or for any rank, grade, part or section of them.   In these traits are found the "ordinances, constitutions and customs," by a wise choice of which the founders of states may, Lord Bacon says, "sow greatness to their posterity and succession."

And now, after a century of growth, of trial, of experience, of observation, and of demonstration, we are met, on the spot and on the date of the great Declaration, to compare our age with that of our fathers, our structure with their foundation, our intervening history and present condition with their faith and prophecy. That "respect to the opinion of mankind," in attention to which our statesmen framed the Declaration of Independence, we, too, acknowledge as a sentiment most fit to influence us in our commemorative gratulations to-day.

To this opinion of mankind, then, how shall we answer the questioning of this day? How have the vigor and success of the century's warfare comported with the sounding phrase of the great manifesto? Has the new nation been able to hold its territory on the eastern rim of the continent, or has covetous Europe driven in its boundaries, or internal dissensions dismembered its integrity? Have its numbers kept pace with natural increase, or have the mother countries received back to the shelter of firmer institutions the repentant tide of emigration? or have the woes of unstable society distressed and reduced the shrunken population? Has the free suffrage, as a quicksand, loosened the foundations of power and undermined the pillars of the state? Has the free press, with illimitable sweep, blown down the props and buttresses of order and authority in government, driven before its wind the barriers which fence in society, and unroofed the homes which once were castles against the intrusion of a king? Has freedom in religion ended in freedom from religion? and independence by law run into independence of law? Have free schools, by too much learning, made the people mad? Have manners declined, letters languished, art faded, wealth decayed, public spirit withered? Have other nations shunned the evil example, and held aloof from its infection? Or have reflection and hard fortune dispelled the illusions under which this people "burned incense to vanity, and stumbled in their ways from the ancient paths"? Have they, fleeing from the double destruction which attends folly and arrogance, restored the throne, rebuilt the altar, relaid the foundations of society, and again taken shelter in the old protections against the perils, shocks and changes in human affairs, which—

> "Divert and crack, rend and deracinate
> The unity and married calm of states
> Quite from their fixture"?

Who can recount in an hour what has been done in a century, on so wide a field, and in all its mnltitudinous aspects? Yet I may not avoid insisting upon some decisive lineaments of the material, social and political development of our country which the record of the hundred years displays, and thus present to "the opinion of mankind," for its generous judgment, our nation as it is to-day—our land, our people and our laws. And, first, we notice the wide territory to which we have steadily pushed on our limits. Lines of climate mark our boundaries north and south, and two oceans east and west. The space between, speaking by and large, covers the whole temperate zone of the continent, and, in area, measures near ten-fold the possessions of the thirteen colonies. The natural features, the climate, the productions, the influences of the outward world, are all implied in the immensity of this domain, for they embrace all that the goodness and the power of God have planned for so large a share of the habitable globe. The steps of the successive acquisitions, the impulses which assisted, and the motives which retarded the expansion of our territory; the play of the competing elements in our civilization, and their incessant struggle each to outrun the other; the irrepressible conflict thus nursed in the bosom of the state; the lesson in humility and patience, "in charity for all and malice toward none," which the study of the manifest designs of Providence so plainly teach us—these may well detain us for a moment's illustration.

And this calls attention to that ingredient in the population of this country which came, not from the culminated pride of Europe, but from the abject despondency of Africa, a race discriminated from all the converging streams of immigration which I have named by ineffaceable distinctions of nature; which was brought hither by a forced migration and into slavery, while all others came by choice and for greater liberty; a race unrepresented in the Congress which issued the Declaration of Independence, but now, in the persons of 4,000,000 of our countrymen, raised by the power of the great truths then declared, as it were from the dead, and rejoicing in one country and the same constituted liberties with ourselves.

In August, 1620, a Dutch slave-ship landed her freight in Virginia, completing her voyage soon after that of the Mayflower commenced. Both ships were on the ocean at the same time, both sought our shores, and planted their seeds of liberty and slavery to grow together on this chosen field until the harvest. Until the separation from England the several colonies attracted each their own emigration, and from the sparseness of the population, both in the Northern and Southern colonies, and the policy of England in introducing African slavery, wherever it might, in all of them, the institution of slavery did not raise a definite and firm line of division between the tides of population which set in upon New England and Virginia from the Old World, and from them later, as from new points of departure, were diffused over the continent. The material interests of slavery had not become very strong, and in its moral aspects no sharp division of sentiment had yet shown itself. But when unity and independence of government were accepted by the colonies, we shall look in vain for any adequate barrier against the natural attraction of the softer climate and rich productions of the South, which could keep the Northern population in their harder climate and on their less grateful soil, except the repugnancy of the two systems of free and slave labor to commixture. Out of this grew the impatient, and apparently premature, invasion of the Western wilds, pushing constantly onward, in parallel lines, the outposts of the two rival interests. What greater enterprise did for the Northern people in stimulating this movement was more than supplied to the Southern by the pressing necessity for new lands, which the requirements of the system of slave cultivation imposed. Under the operation of these causes the political divisions of the country built up a wall of partition running east and west, with the novel consequences of the "border States" of the country being ranged, not on our foreign boundaries, but on this middle line drawn between the free and slave States. The successive acquisitions of territory, by the Louisiana purchase, by the annexation of Texas, and the treaty with Mexico, were all in the interest of the Southern policy, and, as such, all suspected or resisted by the rival interest in the North. On the other hand, all schemes or tendencies toward the enlargement of our territory on the north were discouraged and defeated by the South. At length, with the immense influx of foreign immigration, reinforcing the flow of population, the streams of free labor shot across the continent. The end was reached, the bounds of our habitation were secured. The Pacific possessions became ours, and the discovered gold rapidly peopled them from the hives of free labor. The rival energies and ambitions which had fed the thirst for territory had served their purpose in completing and assuring the domain of the nation. The partition-wall of slavery was thrown down; the line of border States obliterated; those who had battled for territory, as an extension and perpetuation of slavery, and those who had fought against its enlargement, as a disparagement and a danger to liberty, were alike confounded. Those who feared undue and precipitate expansion of our possessions, as loosening the bonds of union, and those who desired it, as a step toward dissolution, have suffered a common discomfiture. The immense social and political forces which the existence of slavery in this country and the invincible repugnance to it of the vital principles of our state, together, generated, have had their play upon the passions and the interests of this people, have formed the basis of parties, divided sects, agitated and invigorated the popular mind, inspired the eloquence, inflamed the zeal, informed the understandings, and fired the hearts of three generations. At last the dread debate escaped all bounds of reason, and the nation in arms solved, by the appeal of war, what was too hard for civil wisdom. With our territory unmutilated, our constitution uncorrupted, a united people, in the last years of the century, crowns with new glory the immortal truths of the Declaration of Independence by the emancipation of a race.

I find, then, in the method and the result of the century's progress of the nation in this amplification of its domain, sure promise of the duration of the body politic, whose growth to these vast proportions has, as yet, but laid out the ground-plan of the structure. For I find the vital forces of the free society, and the people's government, here founded, have by their own vigor made this a natural growth. Strength and symmetry have knit together the great frame as its bulk increased, and the spirit of the nation animates the whole:

> ——"totamque, infusa per artus,
> Mens agitat molem, et magno se corpore miscet."

We turn now from the survey of this vast territory, which the closing century has consolidated and confirmed as the ample home for a nation, to exhibit the greatness in numbers, the spirit, the character, the port and mien of the people that dwell in this secure habitation. That in these years our population has steadily advanced, till it counts forty millions instead of three, bears witness, not to be disparaged or gainsaid, to the general congruity of our social and civil institutions with the happiness and prosperity of man. But if we consider further the variety and magnitude of foreign elements to which we have been hospitable, and their ready fusion with the earlier stocks, we have new evidence of strength and vivid force in our population which we may not refuse to admire. The disposition and capacity thus shown give warrant of a powerful society. "All nations," says Lord Bacon, "that are liberal of naturalization are fit for empire."

Wealth in its mass, and still more in its tenure and diffusion, is a measure of the condition of a people, which touches both its energy and morality. Wealth has no source but labor. "Life has given nothing valuable to man without great labor." This is as true now as when Horace wrote it. The prodigious growth of wealth in this country is not only, therefore, a signal mark of prosperity, but proves industry, persistency, thrift, as the habits of the people. Accumulation of wealth, too, requires and imparts security, as well as unfettered activity; and thus it is a fair criterion of sobriety and justice in a people, certainly, when the laws and their execution rest wholly in their hands. A careless observation of the crimes and frauds which attack prosperity, in the actual condition of our society, and the imperfection of our means for their prevention and redress, leads sometimes to an unfavorable comparison between the present and the past, in this country, as respects the probity of the people. No doubt covetousness has not ceased in the world, and thieves still break through and steal. But the better test upon this point is the vast profusion of our wealth, and the infinite trust shown by the manner in which it is invested. It is not too much to say that in our times, and conspicuously in our country, a large share of every man's property is in other men's keeping and management, unwatched and beyond personal control. This confidence of man in man is ever increasing, measured by our practical conduct, and refutes these disparagements of the general morality.

Knowledge, intellectual activity, the mastery of nature, the discipline of life — all that makes up the education of a people — are developed and diffused through the masses of our population, in so ample and generous a distribution as to make this the conspicuous trait in our national character, as the faithful provision and extension of the means and opportunities of this education, are the cherished institution of the country. Learning, literature, science, art, are cultivated, in their widest range and highest reach, by a larger and larger number of our people — not, to their praise be it said, as a personal distinction or a selfish possession, but mainly as a generous leaven, to quicken and expand the healthful fermentation of the general mind, and lift the level of popular instruction. So far from breeding a distempered spirit in the people, this becomes the main prop of authority, the great instinct of obedience. "It is by education," says Aristotle, "I have learned to do by choice what other men do by constraint of fear."

The "breed and disposition" of a people, in regard of courage, public spirit and patriotism, are, however, the test of the working of their institutions which the world most values, and upon which the public safety most depends. It has been made a reproach of democratic arrangements of society and government that the sentiment of honor, and of pride in public duty, decayed in them. It has been professed that the fluctuating currents and the trivial perturbations of their public life discouraged strenuous endeavor and lasting devotion in the public service. It has been charged that, is a consequence, the distinct service of the state suffered, office and magistraet were belittled, social sympathies cooled, love of country drooped, and selfish affections absorbed the powers of the citizens, and eat into the heart of the commonwealth.

The experience of our country rejects these speculations as misplaced, and these fears as illusory. They belong·to a condition of society above which we have long since been lifted, and toward which the very scheme of our national life prohibits a decline. They are drawn from the examples of history which lodged power, formally, in the people, but left them ignorant and abject, unfurnished with the means of exercising it in their own right and for their own benefit. In a democracy wielded by the arts, and to the ends of a patrician class, the less worthy members of that class, no doubt, throve by the disdain which noble characters must always feel for methods of deception and insincerity, and crowded them from the authentic service of the state. But, through the period whose years we count to-day, the greatest lesson of all is the preponderance of public over private, of social over selfish, tendencies and purposes in the whole body of the people, and the persistent fidelity to the genius and spirit of popular institutions, of the educated classes, the liberal professions, and the great men of the country. These qualities transfuse and blend the hues and virtues of the manifold rays of advanced civilization into a sunlight of public spirit and fervid patriotism which warms and irradiates the life of the nation. Excess of publicity as the animating spirit and stimulus of society, more probably than its lack, will excite our solicitudes in the future. Even the public discontents take on this color, and the mind and heart of the whole people ache with anxieties and throb with griefs which have no meaner scope than the honor and the safety of the nation.

Our estimate of the condition of this people at the close of the century— as bearing on the value and efficiency of the principles on which the government was founded, in maintaining and securing the permanent well-being of a nation—would, indeed, be incomplete, if we failed to measure the power and purity of the religious elements which pervade and elevate our society. One might as well expect our land to keep its climate, its fertility, its salubrity, and its beauty, were the globe loosened from the law which holds it in an orbit, where we feel the tempered radiance of the sun, as to count upon the preservation of the delights and glories of liberty for a people cast loose from religion, whereby man is bound in harmony with the moral government of the world.

It is quite certain that the present day shows no such solemn absorption in the exalted themes of contemplative piety, as marked the prevalent thought of the people a hundred years ago; nor so hopeful an enthusiasm for the speedy renovation of the world, as burst upon us in the marvelous and wide system of vehement religious zeal, and practical good works, in the early part of the nineteenth century. But these fires are less splendid, only because they are more potent, and diffuse their heat in well formed habits and manifold agencies of beneficent activity. They traverse and permeate society in every direction. They travel with the outposts of civilization, and outrun the caucus, the convention, and the suffrage.

The church, throughout this land, upheld by no political establishment, rests all the firmer on the rock on which its founder built it. The great mass of our countrymen to-day, find in the Bible—the Bible in their worship, the Bible in their schools, the Bible in their households—the sufficient lessons of the fear of God and the love of man, which make them obedient servants to the free constitution of their country in all civil duties, and ready with their lives to sustain it on the fields of war. And now at the end of a hundred years the Christian faith collects its worshipers througout our land, as at the beginning. What half a century ago was hopefully prophesied for our far future goes on to its fulfillment: "As the sun rises on a Sabbath morning and travels westward from Newfoundland to the Oregon, he will behold the countless millions assembling as if by a common impulse, in the temples with which every valley, mountain, and plain will be adorned. The morning psalm and the evening anthem will commence with the multitudes on the Atlantic coast, be sustained by the loud chorus of ten thousand times ten thousand in the valley of the Mississippi, and be prolonged by the thousands of thousands on the shores of the Pacific."

What remains but to search the spirit of the laws of the land as framed by and modeled to the popular government to which our fortunes were committed by the Declaration of Independence? I do not mean to examine the particular legislation, State or general, by which the affairs of the people have been managed, sometimes wisely and well, at others feebly and ill; nor even the fundamental arrangement of political authority, or the critical treatment of great junctures in our policy and history. The hour and the occasion concur to preclude so intimate an inquiry. The chief concern in this regard, to us and to the rest of the world, is, whether the proud trust, the profound radicalism, the wide benevolence which spoke in the "Declaration" and were infused into the "Constitution" at the first, have been in good faith adhered to by the people, and whether now these principles supply the living forces which sustain and direct government and society.

He who doubts needs but to look around to find all things full of the original spirit, and testifying to its wisdom and strength. We have taken no steps backward, nor have we needed to seek other paths in our progress than those in which our feet were planted at the beginning. Weighty and manifold have been our obligations to the great nations of the earth, to their scholars, their philosophers, their men of genius and of science; to their skill, their taste, their invention; to their wealth, their arts, their industry. But in the institutions and methods of government; in civil prudence, courage or policy; in statesmanship; in the art of "making of a small town a great city;" in the adjustment of authority to liberty; in the concurrence of reason and strength in peace, of force and obedience in war; we have found nothing to recall us from the course of our fathers, nothing to add to our safety or to aid our progress in it. So far from this, all modifications of European politics accept the popular principles of our system, and tend to our model. The movements toward equality of representation, enlargement of the suffrage, and public education in England; the restoration of unity in Italy; the con-federation of Germany under the lead of Prussia; the actual republic in France; the unsteady throne of Spain; the new liberties of Hungary; the constant gain to the people's share in government throughout Europe; all tend one way, the way pointed out in the Declaration of our Independence.

The care and zeal with which our people cherish and invigorate the primary supports and defenses of their own sovereignty have all the unswerving force and confidence of instincts. The community and publicity of education, at the charge and as an institution of the state, is firmly imbedded in the wants and the desires of the people. Common schools are rapidly extending through the only part of the country which had been shut against them, and follow close upon the footsteps of its new liberty to enlighten the enfranchised race. Freedom of conscience easily stamps out the first sparkles of persecution, and snaps as green withes the first bonds of spiritual domination. The sacred oracles of their religion the people wisely hold in their own keeping as the keys of religious liberty, and refuse to be beguiled by the voice of the wisest charmer into loosing their grasp.

Freedom from military power, and the maintenance of that arm of government in the people; a trust in their own adequacy as soldiers, when their duty as citizens should need to take on that form of service to the state; these have gained new force by the experience of foreign and civil war, and a standing army is a remoter possibility for this nation, in its present or prospective greatness, than in the days of its small beginnings.

But in the freedom of the press, and the universality of the suffrage, as maintained and exercised to-day throughout the length and breadth of the land, we find the most conspicuous and decisive evidence of the unspent force of the institutions of liberty and the jealous guard of its principal defenses. These indeed are the great agencies and engines of the people's sovereignty. They hold the same relations to the vast democracy of modern society that the persuasions of the orators and the personal voices of the assembly did in the narrow confines of the Grecian states. The laws, the customs, the impulses and sentiments of the people have given wider and wider range and license to the agitations of the press, multiplied and more frequent occasions for the exercise of the suffrage, larger and larger communication of its franchise. The progress of a hundred years finds these prodigious activities in their fullest play—incessant and all-powerful—indispensable in the habits of the people, and impregnable in their affections. Their public service, and their subordination to the public safety, stand in their play upon one another and in their freedom thus maintained. Neither could long exist in true vigor in our system without the other. Without the watchful, omnipresent and indomitable energy of the press the suffrage would languish, would be subjugated by the corporate power of the legions of placemen which the administration of the affairs of a great nation imposes upon it, and fall a prey to that "vast patronage which," we are told, "distracted, corrupted, and finally subverted the Roman republic." On the other hand, if the impressions of the press upon the opinions and passions of the people found no settled and ready mode of their working out, through the frequent and peaceful suffrage, the people would be driven, to satisfy their displeasure at government or their love of change, to the coarse methods of barricades and batteries.

We cannot, then, hesitate to declare that the original principles of equal society and popular government still inspire the laws, live in the habits of the people, and animate their purposes and their hopes. These principles have not lost their spring or elasticity. They have sufficed for all the methods of government in the past; we feel no fear for their adequacy in the future. Released now from the tasks and burdens of the formative period, these principles and methods can be directed with undivided force to the everyday conduct of government, to the staple and steady virtues of administration. The feebleness of crowding the statute-books with unexecuted laws; the danger of power outgrowing or evading responsibility; the rashness and fickleness of temporary expedients; the constant tendency by which parties decline into factions and end in conspiracies; all these mischiefs beset all governments, and are part of the life of each generation. To deal with these evils—the tasks and burdens of the immediate future—the nation needs no other resources than the principles and examples which our past history supplies. These principles, these examples of our fathers, are the strength and safety of our state to-day: *"Moribus antiquis, stat res Romana, virisque."*

Unity, liberty, power, prosperity—these are our possessions to-day. Our territory is safe against foreign dangers; its completeness dissuades from further ambitions to extend it, and its rounded symmetry discourages all attempts to dismember it. No division into greatly unequal parts would be tolerable to either.   No imaginable union of interests or passions, large enough to include one-half the country, but must embrace much more.   The madness of partition into numerous and feeble fragments could proceed only from the hopeless degradation of the people, and would form but an incident in general ruin.

The spirit of the nation is at the highest — its triumph over the inborn, inbred perils of the constitution has chased away all fears, justified all hopes, and with universal joy we greet this day.   We have not proved unworthy of a great ancestry; we have had the virtue to uphold what they so wisely, so firmly established.   With these proud possessions of the past, with powers matured, with principles settled, with habits formed, the nation passes as it were from preparatory growth to responsible development of character, and the steady performance of duty.   What labors await it, what trials shall attend it, what triumphs for human nature, what glory for itself, are prepared for this people in the coming century, we may not assume to foretell.   "One generation passeth away, and another generation cometh, but the earth abideth forever," and we reverently hope that these our constituted liberties shall be maintained to the unending line of our posterity and so long as the earth itself shall endure.

In the great procession of nations, in the great march of humanity, we hold our place.   Peace is our duty, peace is our policy.   In its arts, its labors and its victories, then, we find scope for all our energies, rewards for all our ambitions, renown enough for all our love of fame.   In the august presence of so many nations, which, by their representatives, have done us the honor to be witnesses of our commemorative joy and gratulation, and in sight of the collected evidences of the greatness of their own civilization with which they grace our celebration, we may well confess how much we fall short, how much we have to make up, in the emulative competitions of the times.   Yet, even in this presence, and with a just deference to the age, the power, the greatness of the other nations of the earth, we do not fear to appeal to the opinion of mankind, whether, as we point to our land, our people and our laws, the contemplation should not inspire us with a lover's enthusiasm for our country.

Time makes no pauses in his march.   Even while I speak the last hour of the receding is replaced by the first hour of the coming century, and reverence for the past gives way to the joys and hopes, the activities and the responsibilities of the future. A hundred years hence the piety of that generation will recall the ancestral glory which we celebrate to-day, and crown it with the plaudits of a vast population which no man can number. By the mere circumstance of this periodicity our generation will be in the minds, in the hearts, on the lips of our countrymen at the next centennial commemoration, in comparison with their own character and condition and with the great founders of the nation. What shall they say of us? How shall they estimate the part we bear in the unbroken line of the nation's progress? And so on, in the long reach of time, forever and forever, our place in the secular roll of the ages must always bring us into observation and criticism. Under this double trust, then, from the past and for the future, let us take heed to our ways, and, while it is called to-day, resolve that the great heritage we have received shall be handed down through the long line of advancing generations, the home of liberty, the abode of justice, the stronghold of faith among men, "which holds the moral elements of the world together," and of faith in God, which binds that world to His throne.